CELLS

CELLS

JULIA COWAN

www.blkdogpublishing.com

A few words of thanks to those who have helped with this book. To my early readers, who read some chapters and gave valuable feedback and nods of encouragement. A special mention to my colleague and friend, Janet, for reading my first draft and listening to my endless questions and concerns. Lastly, thanks to Lynne for providing a thorough edit. Any help I have received in the last few years on this project has been greatly appreciated.

CHAPTER 1

I woke up in darkness, except for a hazy shape on the wall. Still groggy from what felt like a very heavy sleep, I frantically urged myself to adjust to the lack of light. I had been lying down flat on a thin, musty-smelling mattress, I had no idea for how long, but now I propped myself up, resting on my right arm; I moved slowly, afraid to get up any further. Hesitantly, I extended my arm as far as it would reach into the darkness. I could barely see my hand but there was nothing to touch. The only sound close to me was a deep breathy pant, and it didn't take me long to figure out it was coming from me. When I opened my mouth to speak, my throat felt dry. How long had I been asleep?

'Hello?' I said in a trembling voice which didn't sound like mine. There was no echo. I paused, wanting an answer, but at the same time afraid there would be one.

I blinked several times, in a hurry to clear my vision. As my eyes adjusted to the conditions, I looked to my right and saw there was in fact a single strip of fluorescent light fixed to the wall; this had been the hazy shape I had first seen. Since it was my only source of light, I couldn't tell if this was close to the ceiling or nearer the floor. It gave the small area around it a blueish tinge and emitted a low buzzing sound.

I sat up and then slowly rose to my feet. The mattress, twinned with my fear, made me feel unbalanced. I gingerly placed one foot on the floor, not having to step too far as the mattress was so thin. It felt cheap, and I guessed it was probably filthy. Nervously, I raised my arm and felt behind me. My hand was shaking as I touched a cool, smooth wall. I ran my fingers across it, snail's pace at first and then gradually quicker. Nothing, nothing, nothing. I stumbled slightly, and still frantic, looked down to my feet, even though I was unable to see them. My foot brushed against something; images of giant rats rushed through my mind. But I had only clipped the edge of the mattress. Swallowing hard, I regained my composure and leant against the wall. This was as far as the light would take me; beyond this was only darkness. I was not afraid of the dark, but was not particularly keen on it; mutant spiders and other insects sprang into my head. Slowly, I began edging myself along the wall, using it for support.

Suddenly, I heard a faint crackle before the whole room became illuminated by three lights on the other walls. I could only stare, turning my head slowly to survey my surroundings. I had woken up to find myself locked in a room; this must be a horrific nightmare.

God, this was small, so very small. The room couldn't have been any bigger than a garage, the walls a drab, clay colour. The ceiling was so high that the light didn't seem to touch it. On each wall, about two feet above my head, hung a light strip. I turned 360 degrees to look at the room, quickly at first then much slower. No windows, no doors. How did I get in here? The mattress I had been lying on was pushed against the wall; it was the only piece of furniture in the room. It had probably once been white but now had faint brownish stains on it. I bent down to grasp the edge, in the faint hope that it might be concealing something underneath. I placed my palm on the floor on the area that had been covered. It felt cool. I let the mattress go and it made a dull thud.

'Hello?' I asked again, a bit more quietly this time. My voice did not have to travel very far.

That was it for the room. Nothing else on the ceiling or floor. Nothing else to look at or focus on. Nothing that suggested an exit. I had the bizarre thought of tapping each part of the wall to look for a secret door. Looking down to my feet, I recognised my own battered trainers, laces removed. I was wearing the same clothes I remembered; my last memory was of lying on my own bed, before this nightmare started. Light grey tracksuit bottoms and a blue sweatshirt. Then, out of the corner of my eye, I saw a small metal grille at floor level. I raced to it, threw myself down to floor level more quickly than I intended, so both knees slammed onto the hard concrete.

I winced and opened my mouth in a silent scream before looking through the metal grille. A pencil could probably be passed through each hole, and it was dark on the other side. I placed my palm against it. Was that a breeze I could feel? I hooked my fingers into the grille in an attempt to open it, but it was locked tightly. It must be an air vent. I had visions of green, noxious poisonous gas pumping through it. Too many horror films.

'Hello? Can anyone hear me? Hello?' I shouted into it, since it appeared to be the only exit from this room. I stayed in that position for a few moments, half expecting to see something on the other side, then I sat back onto my feet. There was no way anyone could fit through this grille. How did I get in here?

Just then a voice boomed from the wall behind the mattress.

'Why are you here?' It sounded metallic and almost robotic.

I ran to the wall and stood underneath the light,

my eyes wide, searching for its source. There was a small, white, cylindrical object situated high up on the wall; I guessed this must be some kind of tannoy.

'I… I don't understand...?' I stuttered. 'I'm just here, I woke up here. I don't know how I got here.' I swallowed hard again, trying to dislodge a lump in my throat. I waited for a response, anything.

'Hello?' I repeated, louder. 'I don't know how I got here…' I raised my voice, impatiently.

'Why are you here?' The tinny voiced boomed out again then silence. There was a very long pause. Should I repeat myself again? Could my voice not be heard?

Faintly, I heard a small click. Over and out, end of dialogue. I raced through random thoughts, anything to try to make sense of this question. I struggled to pull together a coherent answer.

Why am I here? Why am I here? I had no idea how I was supposed to reply. I slowly slid down to the floor, my eyes prickling with tears. For the second time in my life, I knew that I, James Hall, scared and alone and aged only seventeen, was in serious trouble.

CHAPTER 2

The house I grew up in was not the best; we weren't rich, but we weren't poor either. We had a big television and other expensive electrical items, for instance, but my mum never seemed to have any money. I lived with her, my dad and my twin sisters in the end house of a row of terraces, on the edge of a moderately sized town. Many of our neighbours, like us, had neglected the front of their house, which made the whole row unappealing. Some had abandoned rubbish outside; they were too lazy to take it to the tip, and it was too large to be taken by the dustbin lorry. Had we have been dumped in a more respectable neighbourhood, our family might have been outcasts, but here we simply blended in. I was sure that this attitude played a big part in our acceptance that this was the way things were and there was no point in trying to change.

My home was not a happy home like you see on TV. I was sure our immediate neighbours suffered from the noise level, and it was probably an advantage that there was no house adjoining the other side. My parents argued all the time, and when they weren't arguing they were shouting. Neither of them had a steady job; Mum looked after the twins and Dad flitted from one job to the next, doing whatever he could, cash in hand.

I remember one of their first arguments. I think I was about four at the time and Dad had come home driving a new car. As it was normal for them to shout, I didn't immediately retreat to my room as another child might have. Swearing had become almost second nature to me. Though I was only four, I understood that this was not our car; and looking back, I can see there was no way we could afford some of the other things we had.

Dad would also disappear for periods of time now and again. He spent some time in and out of prison and when he wasn't inside, Mum would say he was 'on one of his drinking binges' or 'with his fancy woman again'. I began to hate my dad from an early age, as he left us alone to cope and this made my mum cross and angry. When he was home it created tension, and an atmosphere developed as time went on. He was certainly no role model for us. A cigarette hung permanently out of one side of his mouth, and he always seemed to wear the same dirty, grey hoodie. He'd offer me beer and cigarettes, and had a habit of calling me Jimbo; I began to hate this very quickly. He was well known in our neighbourhood for all the wrong reasons. He was feared by the neighbours, but at the same time he was used and respected as someone who could obtain things for them, after taking a small cut for himself.

The first time I felt genuinely scared was just a few years ago. In the very early hours of the morning, I was awoken by an almighty crash from downstairs. I cowered in my bedroom, hands clasped either side of my head making a poor barrier for the sound. We were being raided by the police. My mum argued with them as I did my best to comfort my crying sisters, who had come running into my room. The police went through everything, but found nothing. What a waste of time. Dad wasn't even in.

Then, just over a year ago, Dad disappeared. This wasn't like the other times. My parents were in a rare period of no arguments, so there wasn't any indication he was about to run off. One day he just wasn't there, and I haven't seen him since. I hated myself at first for feeling almost relieved that he wasn't around any more. It meant no more arguments in the house. The feeling soon turned to anger; it seemed all too easy for him to abandon us and start afresh somewhere new.

My sisters, now teenagers themselves, were more than capable of being independent and were only at home sporadically. This meant Mum had no one to look after, and no one to look out for her. She spent hours in front of the television, a drink in her hand, her days long and drawn out like the cigarettes she constantly seemed to puff on. I'd often come home to find her asleep on the sofa, and turn on my heel to head straight out again. I spent time with my friends, hanging out at the park. We'd often drink too, as it became increasingly easy for me to swipe a bottle or two from my mum's ample supply. As a group we were probably quite intimidating, but never had any serious trouble with the police, other than an occasional long look from a passing police car.

This changed. I first got into trouble with the police six months ago. Stupid stuff which quickly escalated to petty theft; I was very lucky to get off with a caution. But did this stop me? You'd hope so, but sadly not. One random Tuesday evening not long ago, I broke into a house three blocks from where I lived. I had become smug and over-confident in the last few months. The crimes I had committed had gone unnoticed by the police. Or maybe they did notice but couldn't link me to anything. I knew that sometimes the police did not even bother to visit the crime scene. In a twist of fate, a friend of mine had his car broken into recently. He complained that he was given a reference number for his insurance and that was all. So I had grown arrogant, and while walking home one night, I spotted an open window at the rear of a house. I scaled the fence easily, but had no intention of trying to squeeze through the window. I had been taught how to pick a lock, and made easy work of the one on the old conservatory door.

However, once I was actually in the house, I wasn't sure why I had broken in. To prove I could? To steal anything I could sell on? My heart was pounding; what if the owner suddenly appeared with a huge baseball bat? Maybe I'd just mess the house up a bit as a wake-up call for them to upgrade their security. I backed quickly out of the door, breathing slowly, watching for the chink of light I expected to see at any moment.

Then, in my haste to get out, I walked into an armchair on the dark, laminate floor. It made a soft, scraping sound, and the movement caused a sideboard to wobble. Quick as a flash, my hand swooped to catch a silver picture frame that would surely have crashed to the floor had I left it. It felt heavy, and I judged that it must be worth a bit of money. I had seen nothing else of any value, apart from a watch and a bit of cash. I was too apprehensive to venture further than the room I was in.

I looked around for anything else that might be worth something. The room I was in was tidy, and decorated with hardwood furniture. If I ran my fingers along any surface, I was willing to bet it they would not show any dirt or dust. A stark contrast to my own house: I could not recall ever having seen either of my parents with a duster in their hand. I concluded that the house probably reflected the family that lived in here: tidy, organised, well-presented.

My eyes fell on a small leather bag neatly pushed against a bookcase. I took one step towards it and spotted that it was personalised with some initials – D.F. It was no use to me and I probably wouldn't be able to sell it, but it felt heavy – the possibility of neatly stacked banknotes sprang to mind. I instantly dismissed this; my imagination was too active for my own good, but I was still intrigued about what was inside. There was a small padlock, which I decided would be easy to break once I got back home.

Out of the corner of my eye I spotted a dog bed. It was empty; the dog could be upstairs and wander down at any moment. My thoughts drifted to my own dog; perhaps I should have brought a handful of biscuits or a string of sausages, like they do in cartoons. I had no intention of being caught, so I decided to leave.

The adrenaline still rushed through me as I retraced my steps. Gripping the handle of the bag tightly, I glanced at the picture in the frame before stuffing it into my pocket. A young girl, probably about sixteen or so, long blonde hair and a pretty smile.

Once out of the house, I headed for the back gate and into the street, then ran, my heart pumping hard in my chest, not glancing back. I took a long way round to my own house before dropping to a slow walk. As I approached my street, my heart rate slowed back to normal, and by the time I was in my bedroom, I was breathing normally. I carefully locked away my stolen hoard, threw my jacket on the floor and lay fully clothed on my bed.

That is the last thing I remember. I sat on the thin mattress, back against the wall. It was stained, as I imagined it would be before the lights had come on, and thin clouds of dust puffed up as I tapped it. I started to feel cold so drew my knees up to my chest and hugged them close to me. I turned my head towards the metal grille wall, thinking that someone could be watching me from the tannoy. I didn't want anyone to see me cry.

One thought played in my head: *why am I here?* Until I could come up with an answer, I was totally doomed. Any possible exit from this place surely depended on that. At the moment, I just couldn't think what to say. I closed my eyes to try to stop the tears. My nose started to run so I used my sleeve and sniffed hard. Wiping my eyes with both hands, I stood up again to carry out my plan of checking each wall. As I walked, I slowly ran my palms along the surface. The walls were solid and made a thick sound as I tapped randomly. I stopped at the metal grille and bent down again. I made a second half-hearted attempt to pry it open. Finding this useless, I resumed my circuit of the room, jumping at several points to check the floor. It was as though the room had been carefully cemented on every surface. Nothing was within my reach; I stretched as high as I could, but couldn't touch the lights.

I sat back down on the mattress, dejected but refusing to believe that there was no escape. I resumed my previous position, rested my head on my folded arms and closed my eyes, thinking of my next steps.

I must have dozed, because I sat abruptly upright as a single sound snapped me from the silence. It came from the direction of the metal grille, low down on the floor. Nothing moved, but there was a definite click. Almost in slow motion, I ran to the wall. It seemed like my feet were struggling through a boggy field.

I knelt again, now at eye level with the grille. A musty smell filled my nostrils, tinged with a subtle aroma of cheese. This immediately made me hungry. I had no concept of time, being entombed in darkness, and no idea how long I'd been asleep. For all I knew I could have missed several meals, or just one. My stomach made a thick, rumbling sound. I put my hand to the grille and pushed my fingers into the holes. It swung gently open. I gasped, and quickly pulled it towards me. Looking down, I could see a tray, which I also pulled towards me. As soon as I let go of the grille, it swung back to its original position. I heard another click and it snapped closed again, like clockwork. As I pulled on it again, I found it was locked tight.

I surveyed what was on the tray: a small cup of water, and on a white plate, a sandwich on white bread, cut lengthways. I raised the top slice and saw two slices of what looked like cheddar cheese. I slowly raised one half of the sandwich to my nose and inhaled warily. The bread was soft and fresh, free of mould. I held the sandwich in front of me and turned it over in my hand. It looked okay; this was enough to satisfy me and I greedily bit into it. A faint thought that it might contain poison entered my head as I chewed on it. I dismissed this quickly. Whoever had put me in here had me captive; what was the point of going to the effort to poison me? I ate the sandwich and downed the water in two large gulps, choking slightly. There was no aftertaste which was a relief. Back home, I was used to eating what I wanted, when I wanted, so this was not a big enough meal, but there was nothing I could do about it. As I placed the cup back on the tray, I looked back at the grille. How was I supposed to return the tray? When was my next meal? Was there going to be another meal? I tried to think why I had been fed, and the only thing that made sense was that I had been captured for a reason. Whoever had put me in here wanted to keep me alive, and needed me to have energy to do… what? There was obviously a purpose for my being here. I just had to figure out what it was.

I picked up the plate and cup again. Both were made of paper, easily disposable and nothing I could make use of. I had a bizarre thought: if they had been made of a different material, I might have been able to make some kind of weapon out of them. Maybe this had been anticipated, so I could not harm myself. I looked down and shuddered; perhaps that was why my shoelaces had also been removed. Disappointed, I shoved the tray away and returned back to the mattress. The next thought to strike me was, if I am being fed, surely there must be some provision for a toilet, unless this was some cruel trick. There was no way a bucket would fit through the grille. My eyes were fixed on the wall. I'd just have to designate a corner, should I need the toilet any time soon.

I didn't want to lie on the mattress so rested my head on my arms. I closed my eyes, not tired but not wanting to stare at the wall any longer. I had dozed for maybe hours, minutes or seconds, but suddenly I jerked upright. A slow, scraping sound came from the metal grille wall, at the top. I stared, mouth agape as a gap appeared, slowly increasing in size. I rose to my feet slowly, watching as it increased to the size of a loft hatch. Then it stopped, as did the noise. In disbelief, I continued to stare as a voice called to me from above.

'Stand back while I lower you a ladder. The Chief wants me to show you something.'

CHAPTER 3

'I want to show you something…' He stood in the doorway of our shed at the bottom of our garden. 'Jim,' he repeated. I knew my father was not a man who liked to wait. It was usual for him to say something once and for it to be done. I sometimes felt glad that I was not the only person to find him intimidating. I had been playing football in the garden for the last few hours, well, maybe not playing, but aimlessly kicking the ball against the wall. I decided to see what he had to show me, honoured to be included in this small detail of his life.

He nodded at me, not smiling, but with a fleeting look of satisfaction. He was wearing a red and white checked shirt, perhaps one of the rare occasions he looked semi-presentable. In the shed, a battered workbench ran the whole length and various tools hung randomly on the walls. They had rusted over the years, and I did not recall ever seeing him with one in his hand. I had a feeling the tools were in the shed already when we bought the house, however long ago that had been.

'Shut the door behind you,' he commanded. 'This

is for your eyes only Jim.' He reached into the drawer of the workbench and carefully pulled out a tea towel. It was bunched up, concealing something. He placed it on the table, then looked at me. Neither of us moved to touch it. I knew straight away that its contents were not good.

'Open it,' he ordered. 'Carefully… but don't touch it.'

I breathed deeply as I unfolded the towel. Inside lay a hunting knife, very new by the looks of it. It had a sharp silver blade and a black handgrip. I stared at it, eyes wide, then looked back at him.

'Now Jim, I want you to clean it. Do it thoroughly, and once you are done, ride your bike into the woods and dump it. I'll be inside when you get back.' That was the end of the conversation.

So I did as he asked. It was not the first time I had helped my dad. It's something I am good at, maybe the only thing.

* * *

I stood at the bottom of the ladder, gazing at the shadowy figure above. It was a man; I was unable to see his face but could tell by his voice. I hastily grasped the ladder.

'Whoa, take your time,' he ordered. 'I think the bottom few rungs are loose, wouldn't want you falling off.'

I slowly placed my foot, testing how strong the ladder was. As I began my ascent, the stranger's face became clearer. The first thing I noticed was his hair; it was a dark blond colour and worn too long for a man, and hung in greasy strands around his face. His eyes were slightly too close together and a long scar ran under one. He must have been in his forties, or possibly older. At the top of the ladder, I allowed myself a look back. The room appeared much smaller from the top. I didn't want to be reminded of it any more so I turned back to the man. He was a few inches taller than me, perhaps less, but through fear or intimidation, I felt unable to stand to my full height.

'Show me your hands,' he instructed.

It took a few moments for this to register. He stared at me, waiting, so I slowly extended my arms and held my hands out, palms up. They were trembling. He looked at me, then grasped one hand, turned it over and pulled it closer to his face. After a closer inspection he let it drop, seemingly satisfied. I frowned, confused.

'Don't even think about trying anything...' My captor held a taser in one hand; he tapped it against his leg and my eyes drifted down. He wore khaki trousers and a short-sleeved white shirt, both perfectly laundered. A bland tie completed the outfit. His clothes reminded me of some kind of security uniform. There was even a space to hang an identification badge, but nothing was attached.

'You need to follow me,' he instructed. I nodded slowly, keen for any information about this nightmare. He motioned with his head for me to follow him. He walked, hand hugging the taser, as if he almost expected me to make a move. His pace was brisk and I tried hard to remember the route, left, right, long corridor, left. The corridors were the same grey colour with small lights fixed on the walls at regular intervals, and the floor was bare concrete. It reminded me of a disused labyrinth that you might pay money to get into in any other circumstances, ready to be spooked at what lay around the corner. There were several thick pipes at ground level, randomly positioned. I vaguely wondered what they were for – air, water, electricity? There was no natural light. Was I underground or was it purposely built like this?

I was led into a small room containing a large desk with a chair on either side. On the desk lay some papers held down by a glass paperweight, a transparent sphere. There was a wooden door opposite the entrance we had just come through.

'Sit, please,' he said.

'Why...' I began, and he held his hand up to

silence me. He sat, and I copied him. He leaned back in the leather chair, narrowing his eyes to look at me.

He steepled his hands in front of him. 'Why are you here?' he asked in a monotone, human now and not robotic like before. This removed some of the fear but I still felt uneasy.

Those words again. What was I supposed to say?

I opened my mouth to answer, but he spoke again.

'Why do you *think* you are here?'

'I... I... don't know...' I began. But my conscience was whispering that this was something to do with my dad. He was well known to the police and could have implicated me in whatever crime he decided to commit; or perhaps I was here as a way to reach him. I swallowed hard, afraid to disclose any of this, and also embarrassed at the prospect of having to describe him to a total stranger. In strangers' eyes, when they find out I am *that* John Hall's son, there is always pity and disgust.

'Have you ever been in trouble? With the police, I mean?'

Light dawned, and I'm sure I paled. I looked down; my hands were gripped tighter than I realized to the sides of the chair. My chair was fabric-covered, fraying in several places. There was one rip on the right-hand side and some yellowish stuffing had begun to poke out.

He glanced at a beige folder on the desk. An A4 sheet lay on top of it, under the paperweight, which he removed and put to one side.

He cleared his throat before speaking, and could have been reading a news report. 'James Hall, break-in at 23 Elm Avenue on Tuesday 13th May. Items taken include a gold watch, silver picture frame, £57 in cash and one leather bag.' He spoke the last three words more slowly, accentuating each syllable. He looked at me. 'These are things that don't belong to you,' he added, as if he were addressing someone half my age.

I swallowed hard. *The break-in.* My dad was not to

blame for this; it had been my own doing. I had been seen by someone, but not arrested. But this was not the police; the incarceration was too harsh.

'Are you working for the police?' My voice was practically a whisper.

He smiled, revealing pale yellow teeth. 'No, *we* are not the police. Police don't treat criminals like this.' He paused then continued, 'How old are you anyway? The file doesn't say. I have a good physical description, brown hair, brown eyes, about five feet nine inches.' He allowed his gaze to travel over me slowly, up and down, as far as the desk would allow.

'Nearly eighteen,' I replied.

His eyes widened slightly. 'How old exactly?' he pressed.

Quickly, I did a mental calculation. 'Seventeen years and five months.'

His stare left me momentarily and drifted off to the left as if he were trying to recall something. My age obviously held some kind of significance.

'Not yet eighteen,' he mumbled. His voice was so quiet I wasn't sure if he was still addressing me or talking to himself. 'I didn't think we were taking them that young…'

I chose not to address why this was an issue for him and changed the subject. 'Who has brought me here? Who has taken me? You said you needed to show me something. Whatever I've done, this isn't right.' My voice trembled. I wanted to scream at him, reach over and grab him by the collar, but I remembered his taser.

He licked his lips and drummed his fingers on the folder in front of him. He spoke slowly, as if he wanted me to take in every word. 'You have been brought to the cell holding facility. You have committed a crime. If you had been arrested, then what? You'd already be out on police bail, ready to offend again. This… is different. While you are here, you are no threat to the public. Really, we are doing society a favour, clearing up the streets, one town at a time…'

I didn't like what I was hearing. 'But… but … this isn't legal; you can't get away with it!' My voice rose and tears filled my eyes again. 'I just want to go home. I'm sorry, I've learnt my lesson…'

'We don't believe that to be true. Your break-in wasn't your first brush with the police…' His tone remained calm.

'That was a while ago. I was stupid and…' My head hung low; I slowly ran my finger over the foam in the chair.

'You won't offend again James, that's for sure. Because if you do, that's it. No more chances. We'll guarantee you don't.' He slowly rose in his chair and walked towards the door behind him. 'I told you the Chief wanted me to show you something. Come with me and you'll see why you'll never offend again.'

CHAPTER 4

He studied me carefully, turning the silver doorknob, then pushed the door open. It seemed heavy, as he used some force. This room was smaller than the one we had just come from, and a large, black leather chair dominated it, facing an array of screens on the wall. Most of the monitors were off, the light reflecting off them creating a small glowing circle. At the bottom left one screen was on; the contrast was slightly too bright but I could make out a dull, coloured image. Below the screens was a large semi-circular desk on which were a series of buttons and a microphone. It looked as though this was the hub of whatever was going on here. Various other paraphernalia was scattered around: a paper coffee cup, a half-eaten pack of biscuits and a few pens in a silver pot.

I regarded the microphone. *'Why are you here?'* The artificial-sounding voice popped into my head, sending chills through me.

'You may sit.' He placed his hand on the back of the chair and swivelled it to face me.

I looked at him before walking over to sit down. It was comfortable and I wondered if this was deliberate; perhaps he whiled away hours studying the screens. He looked back at the monitors.

'Look at the screen,' he instructed, and I focused on the grainy picture. It wasn't the contrast that needed adjusting; the lighting was too bright wherever the image was being transmitted from. I squinted slightly and dared to lean closer. There was what looked like a pile of grey rags on the floor. After a few seconds, it dawned on me that they were not rags; I could just about make out a person, curled up into a foetal position. He lay motionless on the floor; I was unable to see his face as he had a hood pulled over his head and appeared to be using it as a pillow. I realised I was staring, my mouth open with shock.

'What… Who…?' I began. My head snapped round at the man, then back at the screen. 'Is that a person? What is he doing there?' I asked in disbelief, my voice higher than I wanted.

'Meet prisoner number one, James. The person you are looking at was once just like you. He got himself in trouble; he has been given chances but…' His voice filtered off and he shook his head to emphasise his point. 'Sometimes there is no hope, nothing anyone can do. This man spent time in prison, was released and went on to reoffend. So that is where we come in. Like I say, he's been given chances and has not learnt from them. So now he's with us, here.'

He went on, 'So you think the cell you woke up in was like a tomb, bare, with nothing to do, just grey walls to stare at?' It was as though he could read my mind. He smiled. 'Why, that's positively luxurious compared to where this man is. His room is half the size and almost like…' He waved his hand as if he was trying to think of what to say.

'… a well, James. It's like a well. Dark, cold, lumpy, brick walls. Smelly and damp. No one to talk to and we don't talk to him. We're done with talking. He eats, sleeps and that's it.'

'Why don't you just kill him, then? What's the point?' My voice was quiet and tinged with more sarcasm than I had intended.

'We're not *murderers* James.' He practically spat the words. 'We are not that bad. But as I told you, he will never offend again, and if this is what it takes to ensure that, then…'

I breathed deeply and swallowed hard. There was a bitter taste in my mouth. I was aware I was shaking slightly. Fear or shock? I didn't know.

'Is it just him?' I asked nervously. 'And me?'

Without a word, he flicked a switch on the desk and all the screens jumped to life. I let out a small gasp, my eyes not believing what was in front of me. Numerous people, hunched, lying down, pacing, hands and arms flailing wildly. Fists were pounding on walls, floors. Some were shouting, their faces contorted with anger. One looked to be sobbing uncontrollably, the reality of the situation clearly weighing heavily on his shoulders.

'It's probably for the best that there is no volume.' He grinned again. 'The language is not pretty and it's very repetitive. We don't have any kind of conversation with them anyway…'

'Who are they?' I asked.

'*They*? Why James, they are *you*.' His voice rose slightly as he emphasised the last word. 'Not now, but soon. This could be you. With us because it is not fair to have you in the outside world if you are not learning your lesson…'

I slowly shook my head again in disbelief, back and forth to the screens.

'You have a million questions James. Now you've seen what there is to see, let's talk.' He strutted out of the room, and desperately wanting to be rid of the horror in front of me, I followed. We resumed our positions in the desk room.

    'Let me tell you about prisoner number one…'

CHAPTER 5

He leaned back in the chair as he began to talk. 'I've known the Chief since we were young. I met him the day he moved to my street. We played together, went to the same school, college, our parents were close. He was like a brother to me as we were both only children. We've both had tough times in the past and were very close. We *are* very close. He married quite young, and he and his wife quickly had a daughter. She was my god-daughter, and he absolutely doted on her, she could do no wrong. With such loving parents, she thrived.'

I listened carefully, envious of the happy family picture he painted; my early childhood couldn't have been further from this.

'Emily was her name. She had long blonde hair. The Chief was always telling me how worried he was about the day she'd bring back a boyfriend. No boy could be good enough for her. But Emily was clever, and put her school work first. She never let her parents down and he had high hopes for her future…' His voice trailed off.

I realized he was talking about Emily in the past

tense. I didn't like where this was going.

'Emily died when she was eighteen. In fact, she was celebrating her birthday, out with an equally sensible group of friends. She had planned to meet her mum for a lift home, but never arrived at the arranged spot. Her mum was frantic, as it just wasn't like Emily; she was so level-headed and sensible. Her parents searched the area themselves all night, rang everyone they could think of, contacted the police.'

He looked at me solemnly. 'Her body was found a few days later. She had been murdered, her throat cut from side to side.' He imitated the action with his finger. 'The man you saw in the cell on the first screen is her murderer.'

Neither of us said anything for a while. I opened my mouth, but he spoke first.

'Oh they caught him, but the evidence… he was barely in prison before he was released. So you see James, why we were so keen to start this… establishment. People like that need to be dealt with.' He continued, 'this man came out of prison with a smile on his face. It was like he'd got away with it, and he hadn't learned his lesson. He lived in your town and we watched him closely. We saw him laughing with friends in a pub like nothing had ever happened. We saw him leave with different women every other weekend. He went back to his old ways very quickly. So one night, we paid him a visit. He woke up here and has been with us ever since.'

'The question, James, 'why are you here?': he could not give us an answer. He couldn't link his crime with his time here. We ask our inmates here the same question after they wake. Those who are able to answer are taken out and given a second chance. Offend again, you'll be back here, and we don't ask the question again.'

'So what, you spy on people, stalking them?' I asked.

'No we don't need to *watch* people all the time. If

they are released, we fit them with a tracking device…'

My hand instinctively rose to feel the back of my neck, searching for any recent injection or incision. I tried to be discreet but he obviously saw me.

He chuckled, 'you'd never find it…'

I searched for some kind of response to all of this. 'But I didn't answer your question…' I said impulsively, regretting it right away. Maybe he had mixed me up with someone else, someone who did answer the question. I had a sickening feeling I was about to be thrown back into the cell.

'No, I know you didn't,' he replied. 'But like I said, under eighteen is very young. Maybe the Chief saw something in you and thought that an initial visit with us would be enough.'

He looked at me, and his stare made my stomach lurch. 'Then again, maybe not. Maybe you need to spend more time with us as a deterrent.' In that moment I believed him. The way he was dressed and the manner in which he had frog-marched me from the cell told me that he actually enjoyed this.

I spoke quickly. 'So you started this place up because of one man? I'm nothing to do with him, I'm not like that. I'm sorry for the Chief about his daughter, but that's nothing to do with me…' I was almost frantic by now.

'Like I said, we're just clearing up the town, one criminal at a time… Kids like you, this is how it all starts. Prisoner number one deserves to be here because of Emily, and her mother, who could not handle the grief and drove her car into a river shortly after…'

He closed his eyes as if to compose himself.

I trembled, my thoughts racing. Prisoner number one and all the other people I had seen on the screens, bad people, angry and full of hate: that was not me, and I didn't deserve to be here. I felt the room spin, my thoughts in turmoil. I looked at him, eyes still closed, nodding to himself as if this was his coping mechanism for grief. In a blinding impulsive moment, I saw my chance. Without any vestige of a plan, I snatched the paperweight off the desk and threw it squarely towards his head.

CHAPTER 6

The young boy stood on tiptoes, looking through the window. He could barely see out and shifted uncomfortably, transferring his weight from foot to foot, eager to see everything that was going on. His feet were sore from standing in the same position for so long. At night, just before bed, he would often pray, always the same prayer: *please God, let me wake up taller in the morning.* But it never seemed to work. He ate as much dinner as he could every night, as his mother told him that this would help him to grow. The few friends he had at school were already much taller than him. Other boys didn't seem to like him much; he knew he could get angry, and always wanted the toys they had even if he had a perfectly good one in front of him.

His mother picked him up, and they both looked out of the window.

'Can we *please* go out?' he whined for the umpteenth time.

'Not yet,' his mother replied. 'We need to let them at least get all of their belongings out of the removal van first.'

Still, Joe frowned as he looked back at the van. He adjusted his glasses and stared at the main reason he wanted to go out so badly. Riding a small, red tricycle was a boy, probably the same age as him. A new friend.

'Okay, okay.' His mother put him back on the floor. 'Let's see if they need anything. It would be nice for us to welcome them into the neighbourhood.'

A big smile spread over his face. He held his mother's hand as he practically bounced out of the house after her. It was a bright, sunny August day. His mother shielded the sun from her eyes as they approached. A man and a woman were busy passing boxes from the van and carefully placing them on the pavement.

'Hi!' he heard his mother say cheerfully. 'Welcome to the neighbourhood!' She let go of his hand and extended it to them. The woman put down her box and shook it, seemingly relieved at the break.

'Nice to meet you,' she greeted. 'I'm Susan, and this is my husband, Bill.'

Bill wobbled slightly and placed his box by the side of the van. He wiped his brow as he walked over to them. 'We had to pick the hottest day to move in!' he joked.

'I'm Catherine and this young man…' She turned around, as her small son had shyly retreated behind her. 'This is my son, Joseph, Joe for short…'

Susan walked over to him, a friendly, warm smile on her face. She bent down to his level, close enough so she could see her reflection in his glasses. 'Lovely to meet you Joseph, Joe for short. You must meet our son…' She looked around for him; he was peddling towards them.

'David, come and say hello to our neighbours,'

David confidently got off his bike and pumped Joe's hand hard; the adults laughed in unison. Joe stared at the boy while his mother enquired whether they needed anything and pointed in the direction of the nearest shop. He smiled at David, who might become his new best friend. He felt very happy.

***

Sure enough, the two boys did grow up together, very closely. They were both only children. When he was young, Joe didn't know why he didn't have a brother or a sister, but he was in and out of hospital, suffering from various allergies – he seemed to be allergic to everything - so he wondered, as he got older, that if his parents had had another child, would they have been able to look after it as they were so busy with him? He knew why David was an only child just by looking at his parents. They looked *much* older than his. They already had grey hair, and after the day they moved into the neighbourhood, David's father had nursed a poorly back for a while caused by moving the heavy boxes around. 'He will insist on doing everything himself…' he heard David's mother remark.

The boys had spent the rest of that summer playing together, getting to know each other. David enrolled in the same school as Joe, but it was already clear he was much taller; other boys made a beeline for him, seemingly wanting to 'save' him from Joe. However, David was quick to defend his friend and would often go to his rescue. Unfortunately, Joe's appearance, as well as his slim frame and short stature, made him a target for bullies. Large glasses dominated his face and his hair was a mess of strawberry blond. He constantly seemed to be holding a tissue to his nose; hay fever or another allergy meant it ran persistently.

All the same, they lived on the same street throughout their lives, and their parents often socialised together. New restaurant in town? Let's see if the Fosters want to go. New film at the cinema? I bet Susan would like to see that. Football match on? I bet Bill would like to go.

It was clear David was more intelligent than Joe; they attended the same college, only for Joe to drop out after a short while. He struggled to hold down a job that motivated him. He spent time as a bouncer at the local pubs and clubs before drifting off to night security. Patrolling empty offices and warehouses at night seemed to suit him.

One Saturday night David introduced his best friend to his first serious girlfriend, Jill. Joe was embarrassingly captivated by her long blonde hair. He often cursed his bad luck that David had found her first. He wished privately that they would split up, but at the same time he was happy for his friend; but his smile never quite reached his eyes when he saw them together. His jealousy and anger peaked when David confided they were pregnant. They married quickly and had their daughter Emily soon after. As though it was expected of him, Joe, married a few years later and had a son, Karl. Their parents still remained close, and as if history was repeating itself, Joe and David, now living a few streets apart, also remained close. David's career seemed to echo his success at home, as he rapidly worked his way up through the ranks of the police force.

The two of them started fishing together, a chance to escape everything and sit together on a river bank, chatting away for hours, often catching nothing. Joe wondered about his friend and often had guilty thoughts that if he had a wife like Jill, there was no way he would spend hours away from her. Instantly, he told himself off for thinking such things. David was easily his best friend, the only real friend he had ever had. David seemed to have a short temper, and would often become quite animated if they were discussing a subject he disagreed on. He was never violent towards Jill or Emily, but sometimes his outbursts momentarily scared Joe. He just listened, and provided David with someone to sound off to, and often nodded along to placate him whether he shared the same view or not.

He saw this volatile temper during one of their

fishing trips. They belonged to a club, and a prize awaited the person who could land the heaviest catch. This competition was also part of a nationwide event; the cash sum was quite large, and also earned a prestigious title. Joe knew his friend was very much a man who abided by the rules, probably a consequence of his job. David was therefore mindful of the bait they were using, and the rule that it must be the angler who lifts the rod and pulls the catch from the river.

Joe struggled with his rod, and for a few moments it looked as though his fish might get the better of him. After a while, however, he stood at the riverbank with David, extremely pleased with himself as a fellow angler took their picture.

'A good day's work!' David exclaimed. He cast a look skywards. 'I think this might be it for the day, we'll lose the light before too long.'

'Think there might be some sore losers among us,' their new friend explained, handing the camera back to Joe.

'What do you mean?' frowned David.

'Chap up that way.' He flicked his head to the right, further up the bank, where two men sat with their backs to them, their green hats shielding their faces. 'Landed a good catch by the looks of it.'

'Are they cheating?' Joe quizzed.

'Well, not that I've ever done this mind, but I've heard of it being done…' He seemed to be enjoying his captive audience. 'Some people will land a big fish and then shall we say, deliberately increase its weight by seeing what will fit in its mouth or…' He continued, implying that they might have caught a bigger fish elsewhere and put it in the water to create the illusion that it had come from this outing.

David's expression clouded over and his frown turned darker. 'But they can't get away with that…' He took a few steps towards the two men.

Joe sensed his mood immediately. 'Leave it David, we'll raise it at the club. It's not worth it.' He walked up to his friend and took hold of his arms. 'I said leave it…'

David seemed to ponder for a moment and Joe breathed deeply, waiting for him to calm down. When he was satisfied, he released his grip. To his astonishment, David shoved past him and marched towards the men.

'Christ…' Joe muttered to himself, and followed him, sensing he was about to break up a fight. He watched as his friend launched into his tirade, angered further as the two men seemed to be laughing the accusation off.

'Break it up!' Joe attempted to break the scuffle that ensued. The man who had taken their photo helped.

'Christ sake, it's just a competition!' one of the men remarked.

'Pathetic,' the other man muttered, straightening his jacket. His hat had fallen to the floor in the fight and he looked around for it before spotting it on the floor.

David saw an opportunity, and his fist made contact with the perpetrator's face. It caught him off guard but he stayed on his feet and returned the punch. Again, Joe stepped in to try and separate the two, but he could only watch as the other man upped his game. Events seemed to unfold in slow motion; David stumbled backwards and landed with a resounding splash in the murky water.

'Move!' he screamed, panicking. 'He can't swim, he's afraid of the water!' The mood changed as they frantically looked for something to throw to keep him afloat. Joe didn't give it a second thought; he stripped off his jacket, threw it aside slightly more heroically than he meant to and jumped in after him.

He managed to grasp his spluttering and slowly sinking friend, whose fear stopped him from thinking clearly about how to save himself. Joe panted, exhausted, as he held him with one arm and half-paddled with the other. The other man pushed an oar across the surface of the water, and Joe managed to grab it. Together, they worked to pull David safely out of the water. He lay quiet and grey; he had swallowed a lot of water in his panic.

One of the men began an attempt to revive him. Joe could only watch, numb at first as his best friend lay motionless in front of him. Then he shoved the man out of the way; there was no way he could watch from the sidelines while David lay in desperate need of help. He worked to clear his airways of the dirty water, while someone else called for an ambulance. Every second felt like hours. Joe could not revive David, but refused to accept defeat.

'Come on, come on,' he silently willed, 'breathe damn you, this always works on television…' As the siren of the ambulance slowly increased in volume, David began to splutter. He choked up mouthfuls of water and continued to cough when there was none left, struggling to compose himself.

Joe sat back, resting on his feet. Relief washed over him. He swallowed a lump in his throat, and fought down an overwhelming urge to cry. Relief? Compassion? He wondered whether he would feel the same way if he had just saved the life of a total stranger. He allowed the paramedics to take over and stood back, clothes heavy and sodden with the foul-smelling water.

Following the all clear from the hospital, he took David home. David had insisted on Jill not being called.

'I just fell into the river, I'm okay,' he tried to reassure her, still shaken by his ordeal. 'I'm fine, Joe helped me…'

'Thank God.' Jill hugged Joe hard. 'Thank you,' she whispered.

When they had all calmed down, they sat in David's back garden as they often did. They were both fortunate enough to have large gardens and often spent the long summer nights, drinks in hand, talking about anything and everything. After a while Jill went to see to

Emily, who had just woken from a sleep. The two men heard her comforting the little girl over the baby monitor.

'You saved my life,' David stated solemnly to his friend.

They looked at each other and Joe smiled, almost embarrassed. He was sure David would have done the same thing if the roles had been reversed.

'And I won't forget this,' David added.

* * *

Marriage seemed to suit David, but tragedy struck hard for Joe. He and his wife drifted apart and eventually divorced when their son was young. This almost seemed to emphasise Joe's pangs of jealousy towards his friend and his apparently perfect life.

'You work so hard,' Jill complained to her husband. They were sitting in Joe's back garden as the evening drew to a close. It had been warm enough to eat outside and now they relaxed, drinks in hand.

David shrugged off his wife's comment. 'What can I do?' he joked. 'People keep committing crimes, keeps us all busy...'

He was interrupted by a heavy knock on the front door. Joe checked his watch, puzzled. 'Who at this time...?' he muttered, setting down his beer and heading through the house to answer the door.

Time passed and David somehow sensed that all was not well. 'I'll just go and check...' He rose and Jill followed, concerned. They walked through to the lounge, where a crumpled figure awaited them. David frowned as he recognised some of his colleagues, while Jill, without hesitation, went to comfort Joe.

'There's been an accident...' David's colleague took him to one side. 'A car was struck by a speeding vehicle...'

David listened in a blur. His best friend's family

had been wiped out in the blink of an eye. Joe sat numb, tears pouring down his face, unable to take in the details of his ex-wife and son's death. Jill sat by his side with her arm around him, her presence enough to console him a little.

He found he relied on her more and more as the trial began of the man responsible for the accident. 'They will get what they deserve,' Jill would whisper to him. Six months later their affair began; they both felt guilty for betraying David, but that didn't stop them taking advantage of his erratic work patterns.

He often pressed her for an answer to when she would leave David for him, but he knew he had to be patient – she needed to get Emily through school first.

He held her hand tightly as they sat in the public seating area of the court. Joe studied the smirking, uninterested defendant and looked at him with contempt. When the verdict of 'not guilty' was announced, he pushed Jill away and slammed his fists down on the chair beside him. Anger simmered away inside him.

A short time later, David made the discovery that would change the course of their lives forever.

* * *

It was a rare Saturday that David was not on a weekend shift. He had planned to go out for a day's fishing with Joe, as Jill had already made plans. He was aware that he needed to spend more time with his friend; the death of his ex-wife and son were still devastating to him and he felt that he had not been there for him as much recently. He wandered around the house that morning, having promised to tidy up a bit. Emily was also out so he was able to work more slowly than if anyone else had been in. In the process of making the bed, out of the corner of his eye he spotted something under it. He frowned as he bent to pick it up. He picked up a silver chain and instantly knew whom it belonged to. His hand trembled, and he sat for a while on the edge of the bed, desperately trying to think of a rational explanation for how something belonging to his best friend was in his bedroom. *This must have fallen off when he'd helped her look for something, or he had been helping her to move some furniture. Maybe it's a gift for me and it just so happens that it is the same one Joe has…* A knock on the door snapped him from his thoughts and he calmly walked down the stairs to answer it.

'What's happened? You look as if you've seen…'

He waved Joe in but could not bring himself to make eye contact with him. The one conclusion about the silver chain that he hadn't wanted to face hit him. Were the two of them involved in some way? The more he thought about it, the more ridiculous this notion seemed. His *wife* and *best friend*. However much he tried to push it out of his mind, this rotten, twisted thought crept back in. So he forced himself to question it. Did I miss the signs? he asked himself. All the time they've spent together? Did I miss the looks they gave each other?

'Tell me what's been happening between you and my wife.' He felt relatively composed but knew that this could change at any moment.

Joe wrestled with his thoughts for a moment, but deep down he was relieved. *I wanted him to know… no more secrets. He knows, so there is no point denying anything.*

'How long…?'

'I…I don't know…' He searched for an answer.

'I said *how long*?' David's rage was now rising to the surface. He was renowned for his temper, but over the years he had worked on staying composed and in control. Now when he was angry, he only had to raise his voice to put the fear of God in the recipient. Joe had never seen this side of his friend directed at him before. He had shuddered at the memory of one evening when he had collected David from work as they had arranged to meet for a few drinks and had witnessed him giving a colleague a dressing down, his voice low and menacing.

'Not long after the funeral,' he stated, simply. There was no point in lying.

'Do you love her?' he asked, bitterly.

'Yes, I do...'

'And do you expect her to leave me for you?' David demanded. 'Because I won't let her go. I'd see you dead first.' His voice was cold, and the anger welled up inside him. He looked up at Joe, disgusted at his betrayal. His rage simmered to the surface and reached boiling point. When he could not contain it any further, he took two steps forward and threw the first punch.

Joe stumbled backwards and crumpled to the floor. Somehow, that punch made him feel real again, brought him back to life. He sat, panting, holding the side of his face, which was beginning to throb. He hoped there would be no more punches. 'There is no excuse for what I've done,' he said, leaning against the wall. 'I've loved her for a very long time and she was there for me after... I took advantage...' This wasn't exactly true but there wasn't any need to explain any further. Suddenly, every feeling he had tried so hard to suppress since the death of his family came rushing to the surface. He felt the tears he had fought so hard to suppress prickle his eyes.

'You've no idea...' he sobbed, 'what it's like seeing the scum that ruined your entire life walking around, getting on with his own life as if nothing happened while I'm left with nothing. I'm the one with the life sentence... You, you work for the system that helped get him out of prison, left him to walk the streets...'

'I just want them to pay for what they've put me through,' he continued. He dared not get up, fearing further blows, and drew his legs up in case David decided to throw in a few kicks too. 'They don't deserve to live. At the very least, they should be locked up and the key thrown away.'

David slowly paced around the room, in deep thought. He thought of the times in the past that Joe had been there for him. Now was not the right time to punish him and show the full force of his wrath. Something had been playing on his mind for some time, a thought he could not shake, and now he had the perfect opportunity to speak of it. It was something he had wrestled with in his professional capacity for a while. Finally, he spoke. 'I can help you but you also need to help me,' he explained. 'I will help you make him pay, but on the condition you never see my wife again.'

* * *

They drove in silence out of town, through quiet winding country lanes. They had travelled a long way before David steered the car off the road and onto a muddy track.

'We walk from here.' He was not sure if the car would take them any further, and he also feared leaving identifiable tyre prints in the fresh dirt. He stopped the car and got out. 'I want you to follow me.' He walked towards a large steel building. The door creaked loudly as he pushed it open. Winding, narrow corridors lay ahead, and a metal flight of stairs led to an observation area. A dusty smell greeted them and the humid air moved around them.

'This was some kind of factory,' David explained. 'It has been unused for a while now. This area overlooks the ground floor...' He switched on a light and illuminated the entire floor space. 'It needs some work to make it... useable again. There is plenty of space to expand underground; we can build storage rooms and possibly even a section containing living quarters.'

He looked through the window which was opaque with dirt, and rubbed a small section with his fist. Joe could make out a large area with support beams dotted around the floor.

'What is your plan?' Joe asked, curiously but wary.

'This will be a prison,' David said. 'Our prison. This is my way of helping you. I see so much every day, criminals getting away with their crimes and not showing any kind of remorse. You've no idea what it's like in my job. We do our utmost to catch a criminal, make the best case when they go to court only to see the whole system collapse. Cases crumble on a technicality, or the judge passes a ridiculous sentence. So many criticisms: prisons aren't tough enough, police are too soft on crime. I'm working my hardest to ensure that isn't the case, but the system lets us down. You've said it yourself, Joe. We'll build this for purpose and when we're ready, we'll move everyone in who was responsible for Amanda and Karl's death. You're right, they should be in prison, but any ordinary prison is too good for them. They'll stay here, with us, until the day they die. They'll know what real suffering is like.'

'When I said you'd never see Jill again, I meant it. I could have killed you when I found out, I won't lie to you. But maybe I owe you something, after how you've helped me in the past. It will be your job to live on site and oversee... our guests. Treat them as you wish,' he concluded, dourly.

Joe swallowed hard, composing his response. 'But... but... your position in the force,' he stuttered. 'You're risking everything...'

He paused for a while. 'Let me worry about that. I know a few people who owe me some favours shall we say. I can get help from people without them knowing directly what they are involved in. Besides, is what I am doing so wrong?' he retorted. 'These people are criminals already. All I'm proposing we do is punish them properly in a way that our courts are unable to do. So many people exploiting loopholes, being let off on a technicality, witnesses unable to give full evidence in fear of reprisals. Do you want me to go on?'

Joe shook his head, unable to support or condemn the plans set out in front of him. He listened, wide-eyed, intrigued but unnerved by his friend. This was a man he didn't ever want to cross. For the first time since the day they had met, he had seen him in a new light; he genuinely felt afraid of him.

CHAPTER 7

'Happy birthday.' She smiled at him broadly, proud of the gift she had placed in front of him. It had taken her a while to save up for it but she'd spotted it a while ago and knew that this was what she wanted to get her father for his birthday.

'Thank you Emily,' he replied, puzzled at the size of the present. He hadn't seen her bring it down from her room with the other gifts she had bought him – a gold pen and a novelty tie. It had become a family tradition for her to buy him the most hideous tie she could find for every occasion. Christmas was usually good for garish ties; that was when it had started, but now Emily had extended it to his birthday. There was also a condition: he had to wear it. This year's had several large pigs scattered down the length of it. As he normally dressed smartly, these ties were a contrast and often served as a source of amusement for the family.

He regarded the present now in his lap. It was wrapped in gold paper with a neat bow fastened to the top. It was a medium-sized cuboid and relatively light.

'I take it this isn't another tie then…' he asked quizzically.

'No, just open it.' Emily could not understand why her father preferred to guess every conceivable possibility rather than just open the thing. It often irritated her to the point where she contemplated taking the gift away until he promised to guess sensibly or simply unwrap it.

'Not a tie, not a football…' He threw in one final quip. 'Okay, okay…' he added as he fumbled with the bow. Her mother had a policy of reusing gift-wrapping paper, and Emily knew that her father was taking his time to avoid damaging it. At Christmas, one of her relative's presents would be in this same paper.

David unveiled the gift, and in front of him sat a tan leather holdall. He opened his mouth in surprise as he ran his fingers over the monogram on the side – D.F.

'So, do you like it?' she pressed.

'It's gorgeous.' His eyes welled up and he knew he was showing slightly more emotion than he usually did in front of her. He was so touched to receive such a present from her. The brown leather was well polished; it would have taken many shifts at her job in the local supermarket to raise the funds for it.

'Emily, I love it. Come here.' He pulled her into a clumsy embrace and the bag was squashed between them.

'Are you sure you like it?' she asked. 'I thought you could use it for your trips away. Look, it's got lots of compartments inside, and it's smarter than the one you insist on dragging round with you at the moment…' Her fingers separated the cloth inside and she put her hand in each space to test its depth.

'I'll take it everywhere I go,' he reassured her. 'This will never leave my side.' He patted it proudly.

CHAPTER 8

I backed quickly out of the door, keeping my eyes on the unconscious man the whole time. He sat slumped in the chair with his eyes closed. The paperweight had been more effective than I'd imagined. A thin stream of blood ran down from the top of his head. Was he dead or just knocked out cold? I didn't know, and did not wish to wait and find out. I turned out of the room and half walked, half stumbled. A sharp pain shot up my leg as my ankle momentarily gave way. I silently cursed, testing whether I could bear weight on it before I limped out of the room. I had no plan, but being away from him was a start. I mentally scolded myself when I came to the end of a corridor; I was not remembering the route. Then I saw it – the ladder that I had climbed up not so long ago. Allowing myself a quick glance into the hole, I saw the dirty mattress on the floor. That was enough to convince me that this had been my cell. I recalled when I first climbed the ladder, I had turned left. As I had just come from that direction, I chose to carry straight on.

Round the corner it looked no different; I might

just as well have walked down the same corridor again. There was nothing to distinguish it, just another long grey corridor and two more at the end branching left and right. I stopped to look back. Why was the ladder I had climbed still there? Why hadn't one of the 'workers' or 'The Chief' come to remove it? I realised that I wasn't being observant; there was the possibility I would run into someone who would be ready to throw me back into the cell. What would I do then? I had nothing to defend myself with.

At the end of this corridor was a plain white door. With my ankle still throbbing, I ran the best I could towards it, and to my surprise, it opened. Inside, there were two metal shelving units, one on either side. The shelf closest to the door had many loaves of white bread stacked neatly. Next to them, rows and rows of boxes of processed cheese were carefully stacked on top of each other. The other shelf was home to boxes which were labelled 'cups' and 'plates' in black marker pen. I half expected to see bottles of water on one of the shelves but there were none. At the end of the shelves was another door, also white and closed. Thoughts raced through my mind: was I spending too much time looking around instead of looking for an escape route? This door might be the way out; I turned the handle and it opened.

It was clear the room was being used by someone to sleep in. Pushed against the wall was a single bed, made up with a green blanket carefully tucked in under the mattress. It didn't look very comfortable and reminded me of an army bed. A wardrobe stood next to it, and a desk and chair next to that. I concluded that this room was being used by just one person. There was one other door in the room. It also opened, to reveal a toilet, sink and shower. I looked in the mirror and gazed at my reflection. I didn't recognise myself. My skin already seemed pallid from the lack of light; my eyes had dark circles around them and my face looked dirty. I hastily splashed water on my face and took several gulps from the running tap. As I backed out, my focus was centred on the toilet. *Get out of here, James!* But my urge to use the toilet was too great. I stood, willing myself to go faster. The toilet seat slammed shut, causing me to momentarily freeze. Expecting to hear footsteps at any moment, I quickly left the bathroom.

I'd found someone's bedroom. It panicked me to think whoever slept in here could walk in at any moment. With my hand on the door, I stopped. I turned and dared myself to walk to the desk to get some clues to whom this room may belong to. There were three pictures on the desk; two men stood smiling in one. It was a framed newspaper clipping and looked as if it had been taken after a successful fishing trip; they both stood proudly holding up prospective catches. The newspaper headline screamed out at me, 'Bakerfield's Best Catch!' I looked closely at the men; I didn't recognise one of them, but the other man was *him*, my captor, Mr Greasy Hair, who was currently slumped in a chair not far from here. I smiled at the nickname I had given to him. He looked much stockier in this picture, and his dirty hair was much shorter and tidier. I peered closer; there was no scar under his eye.

The second picture was of the man who next to Mr Greasy Hair in the first one; here his arm was draped over the shoulders of a woman. I couldn't place her but had a feeling I'd seen her somewhere before.

The last picture made my blood run cold; I recognised the girl in this picture straight away. It was the exact same print I had stolen during the robbery. It was Emily. That was when it occurred to me: James, I told myself, I think this is the Chief's room.

CHAPTER 9

They sat in the car, watching people enter and leave the pub. It was just about closing time and the area was getting louder by the hour, men and women drunk after a late night. Joe sat in the passenger seat. On his lap rested a beige folder, which David had given to him when he'd got into the car, but he was yet to open it.

David was used to surveillance, but this was a new experience for Joe. He was used to moving around on a job, and hours of sitting down began to prove uncomfortable for him. David seemed to sense this, and said, 'Subject A is currently in the pub. It's not that long until closing time.' He checked his watch. 'He lives about half a mile from here and usually walks home.'

Joe began to flick aimlessly through the notes in the file. There was a collection of black and white photos of the man they were looking for. In all of them, he was unaware and going about his daily life. Of course Joe recognised him; for he had sat stiffly in the court throughout his trial; his cheap suit had failed to provide any kind of disguise, for he knew the type of man he was.

Subject A was Steven Jones, aged 28. He had been behind the wheel of the car that had ploughed into the path of his innocent ex-wife and son. This man had sat in court, stifling yawns at times, showing no remorse for his actions. His previous convictions were printed neatly on a sheet of A4 paper, and almost reached the bottom, surprising for someone of such a young age.

'Do you know anything else about him?' he mumbled to David, still engrossed.

'Broken family, no real job to speak of. Father also in and out of jail… usual thing, I see it all the time.'

'Like father, like son eh?' remarked Joe. 'What a start in life to give your kids. He never stood a chance…'

'Don't feel any pity for him,' replied David, bitterly. 'It was entirely his decision to sit behind the wheel that night, drunk and high on drugs. And his two friends in the car, in the same condition but did nothing to stop him driving off. Believe me, I'm preparing dossiers on them as we speak…'

Joe nodded. This was to be justice for Amanda and Karl in the most extreme form, on their terms.

'There's our man.'

Joe sat up straight now, following his friend's gaze. His mind had briefly begun to drift back to Jill, as it tended to do when he found himself with time to think. The last few months had been very busy for the two men; there was plenty to keep them occupied, getting their prison up to speed. He hadn't seen her since the day David had found out the truth about their affair.

'Do we follow?' he asked, puzzled.

'Not yet,' David replied. 'We'll see that he gets home, then pay him a visit later tonight.'

'And which… cell will he be put in?' Joe enquired.

David thought for a moment. 'This particular individual can go in the well. There's no chance of him coming out. But we'll still implant the tracking device and monitor him. You'll want reminders that this is all worth it.

Don't feel any pity for him.'

Joe nodded in agreement. 'And the other subjects? His friends?'

'As I say, I'm gathering information on them at the moment. We'll decide which cells to put them in once we're up and running.'

'Just out of interest,' Joe asked, 'we're building the facility for a dozen… inhabitants…'

'We'll concentrate on this case first and then…' He paused. 'Well, I'm sure the town will benefit immensely from having career criminals removed from the streets…'

***

Joe walked through the corridors slowly, his solitary footsteps echoing off the walls. In the storage cupboard he arranged a few boxes, shifting some from one shelf to another. He began to whistle as he retrieved a tray and proceeded to gather the ingredients he needed: bread, butter, cheese and a cup of water. Why am I being so generous with the cheese? he thought. But by now, his routine had become established; three meals a day, the same cheese sandwich on a plate, accompanied by a cup of water. He looked at the somewhat meagre portion, and recalled a conversation he'd recently had with David. 'I don't want him to die of hunger,' he'd said. 'Where's the justice in that? He won't be with us for very long if he starves to death.'

David had nodded in agreement. 'What do you propose?' Joe replied, 'Hmm, I'm not sure. Perhaps a supplement of some kind? I'll look into it. In the meantime, I'll make the portion sizes bigger.'

He balanced the tray carefully in one hand and went out of the door, closing it behind him. He took the usual route: along the corridor and down the steps, into the musty darkness. There was a strong aroma in the air of the basement area, thick and repellent. Bending down to floor level, he reached for the button on the side of the grille. This had become a swift movement that he had perfected over time, activate the button and push the tray into the space in between the cell and the outside. He could do it so that the prisoner did not have enough time to get to his side of the grille before he'd deposited the tray and slammed the grille shut. I don't want any contact with him, he reminded himself.

The button was fully depressed, but this time he did not hear the click which signified the grille was open. He pressed it again, then several more times. Stuck. There was no way he would be able to repair it with no access to the other side. He nudged the grille and found it open. I think he's wedged it open somehow on the other side, he thought. Is he deliberately sitting there, waiting, knowing when to expect the next meal? Frowning, he pushed the tray inside.

The voice on the other side made him jump. 'Let me out of here!' Steven, whom they referred to as subject A, growled at him, 'When I get you, I'll kill you! I've got friends and we'll get everyone who knows you but I'll take great pleasure in killing you myself…'

Joe composed himself and breathed deeply. 'No, you won't,' he taunted. 'There's no way out for you. We've got you now. And your friends? We'll get to them first…' He smirked to himself.

Their eyes met, and anger blazed through the man on the other side of the grille. They held each other's gaze for a while, waiting to see who would break first. Joe smiled, ignoring the torrent of abuse that followed. He slammed the grille shut and made his way back up the stairs.

* * *

He watched Subject A's cell carefully, monitoring any changes. Following their conversation, he'd begun to kick the walls randomly. He screamed up to the tannoy, demanding an answer. Joe watched as other cells began to fill up, until they were both satisfied that everyone who had played a part in the fatal crash was now there.

He was aware he had reached the point of no return long ago; there was no way he could pull out of this arrangement, no way he could shift the guilt if they were discovered. It gave him a certain sense of power, however, under the watchful eye of David, 'The Chief', as he now called himself. True to his word, Joe stayed at the facility whilst the Chief visited regularly and they discussed how everything was progressing. Joe felt his confidence grow in his new role; he even allowed himself visits away from the facility on nights when he knew all the inhabitants were settled and fed. He would visit his home town and meet up with old friends... In a courageous and daring move, he even allowed himself the luxury of contacting Jill. She was, of course, pleased to hear from him. She appeared not to know David had found out about them, and he decided not to tell her; instead he arranged to meet her in hotels and pubs where they knew they would not be discovered.

Their plan for their facility was relatively simple – when a new arrival was placed into a cell, unconscious and with no recollection of how they had got there, Joe would record their movements and then make recordings. This might serve a purpose later on; he wasn't sure what as yet but it did give him a kind of satisfaction, playing out these tapes on the long nights, seeing these prisoners at their most vulnerable and desperate state.

'You got what you deserved,' he would often whisper, to himself, as they had no way of hearing him. They had a strict rule: absolutely no communication with them at all, apart from the initial questioning. Do not feel any pity and do not engage in any kind of dialogue.

Twelve prisoners now found themselves in their facility. Joe did not take any part in transporting them here from their homes in the night. He did not want to dwell on how the Chief did it. He often scanned the newspapers for any stories which expressed suspicion about the disappearance of so many people from one town. There did not seem to be any. People move in and out of towns every day, he told himself, and since they were not exactly model citizens, others were probably grateful they had left.

They had installed cameras in the cells, and Joe often found himself staring at the screens for hours. It was fascinating to see the different reactions; some of the captives screamed endlessly, others seemed to accept their fate and sat silently, waiting. The walls had been carefully plastered, by Joe himself, but some even seemed to think they could claw their way out.

Joe looked carefully at one of the screens. There was a particular prisoner who had been hunched over the side of the mattress for some time. Every now and again, he leaned back against the wall, mouth agape.

The Chief walked in and Joe acknowledged him.

'I think this guy is sick,' he explained.

The Chief leaned on the desk, studying the screen. 'Boy it's going to stink in there.' He pulled a mocking face. 'Is he the only one? Anyone else sick?'

Joe shook his head. 'Not that I can see...' He leaned back in his chair, choosing his words carefully. 'Listen, I wondered whether...'

The Chief looked at him, still standing over him, almost intimidatingly.

From under the desk, Joe retrieved a small box. 'Can I... I mean, would it be okay if you gave this to Emily? For her birthday I mean?' He stuttered, 'she's... she's only eighteen once. I wanted her to have it, even if I don't get to give it to her...'

Without a word, the Chief took it from him. For one moment, Joe thought he would be scolded for leaving the facility. However, the Chief must have known that this condition would not be enforceable. He had to have a life outside of this place, surely?

'I'll see that she gets it.' There was never any kindness in his voice when it came to discussing his family with Joe. In fact, he did not talk about them in his presence. He stood up straight again and turned to leave.

'By the way, I've said it before, you are not to leave this place for any reason. We had an agreement. Do you understand?'

Joe nodded, slightly taken aback. He watched him leave, then turned back to look at the screen again. A thought ran through his mind. *We are all prisoners; some walls are wider apart than others.*

CHAPTER 10

I had absolutely no plan about what to do next. It had seemed tempting to stay in the room, but there was the threat that someone would come in; this was an area which the Chief probably visited regularly, and if he was on the premises, he could return at any moment. Also, being on the move might mean that I could find an exit. Searching through the drawers and wardrobe had revealed nothing out of the ordinary. Rows of identical shirts and trousers were hung neatly in the wardrobe and socks, underwear and t-shirts were precisely folded in the drawers. I idly wondered how clothes were washed here. Perhaps there was another room I had not yet encountered, which contained a washing machine. This seemed plausible; I could picture a small room containing a single appliance set innocently at the back of the room. Maybe there would also be a drying rack with rows of socks hung to dry.

I walked slowly and carefully along the corridors; I didn't want to make a sound and I wanted to take in every piece of information. But there was nothing to see, only grey walls and the lights buzzing quietly. My shoes made a faint scraping sound on the floor.

I encountered a locked door before reaching the end of the corridor, and jiggled the handle a few times before giving up. At the next corner, the sight in front of me caused me to stop in my tracks. It was a door but this one was ajar: the only open door I had come across since leaving the Chief's room. Had I just walked in a circle? I frantically tried to remember the colour of the door I had run out of without giving Mr Greasy Hair a second glance; did I close it after I left? Or was this the door to the storage room which led to the Chief's room? I dared not go any closer, in case he had regained consciousness and lay waiting for my return, weapon in hand. *Christ James, get a grip and get moving!* I chided myself. The handle felt cold and heavy in my hand. Slowly, I pushed the door fully open.

The chair had an imprint in it that indicated someone had recently been sitting there, but it was empty. It was swivelled parallel to the desk, as if someone had staggered out of it. The spherical paperweight lay against the skirting board. I dared myself to look behind the desk, half expecting to see a figure on the floor, sprawled out, ready to have a chalk mark drawn around it. The floor was bare though; there was just the thin, brown carpet, worn in several places, which covered the floor. I jerked around quickly enough to cause a sharp pain in my neck, expecting to see him standing over me ready to strike, eyes bulging, teeth clenched.

The room was empty.

I picked up the paperweight, which had rolled over and was now resting on the skirting board; it had served as a weapon before so it could be useful again. I didn't want to hurt him, just threaten him with it so he would let me go. I'm not like them, I told myself. I hadn't intended to throw it before, and had done so without thinking. Maybe I should have let him continue to talk; perhaps he was about to release me. On the other hand, the fact that he had given me something to eat suggested he was not quite done with me yet.

The door to the screen room was ajar, so I gingerly edged the door open and found it empty as well.

I sat on the leather chair again, and prepared to look again at the screens. The images that had haunted me before were still being transmitted. Prisoner number one had changed position and was now sitting up, hunched over as I had been, on his probably filthy mattress. I wondered what was going through his mind. Had he accepted his fate or was he secretly plotting his escape? It didn't bear thinking about, the sense of entrapment and utter helplessness that must be in his mind.

I scanned the other screens, and watched the other prisoners. I focused on the screen directly in front of me; the man it showed was pacing in a small circle, hands on top of his head. I stared, hypnotised – then I saw a small jump on the screen. I gasped and leaned back slightly, trying to see the screen more clearly, and shook my head. Had I seen a jump? Had I imagined it? If I had, what did it mean? I continued to stare, and he continued to pace steadily, as if he was being operated remotely, never stopping or slowing down. I willed him to move differently, to change course from what I was seeing.

Then, after a few minutes, the jump again.

He paced steadily in front of me… he moved as if he was programmed… and then the jump.

I felt physically sick as it dawned on me. This was not a live feed. I was watching a pre-recorded tape.

I trembled with fear as I studied each screen, desperate to see something, anything, my eyes darting from one to the next, hungry for information. My fingers pressed against the edge of another screen; Mr Shouting Man, as I'd dubbed him, faced directly towards the camera, his face twisted with anger. The gap between jumps was much longer this time, maybe about five minutes, but it was difficult to judge. What were these tapes? What purpose did they serve? I counted fifteen screens in total, Prisoner number one was in the bottom row on the right. I concentrated on him for a few minutes, and became convinced that his feed was live, happening at this moment. I scanned a few screens along from him and gazed at another prisoner. This man was barely visible, and sat by the far wall, I guessed facing the tannoy wall. His movements were sporadic; he had moved his mattress near the metal grille and I concluded he might well be asleep.

I pushed the chair back as far as I could, and it came to rest against the wall. I dropped to the floor under the desk, not sure what I expected to see, or indeed what I was looking for. There was a wooden sliding cupboard door underneath, and it opened smoothly. Inside, stacked on top of each other in neat rows, stood fifteen video players. It took me a few seconds to work out that they were not DVD players, which I was used to. I ran my fingers over the front of one. How old was this place, to have such dated equipment? I counted twelve lights; I had been watching twelve recordings. I pressed a pause button on one and looked up at the screens, and sure enough one of them froze.

I sat back on the chair, confused about the logic behind this. When I worked out which player matched which screen, it led me to believe the only live images were the empty cell I had woken up in, Prisoner number one and Mr Sleeping Man. Just three prisoners, or inmates, or whatever he called them. Just three. I couldn't make sense of any of it. Where were the people on the tapes? Why were there only three live feeds? What kind of dangerous man was Mr Greasy Hair if he was prepared to set up an illusion like this?

I chewed on my thumbnail as I watched Mr Sleeping Man, unsure what to do next. Suddenly he jerked awake, and I jumped back. He sat upright, and I could see him more clearly. He wore a grey hooded top and I could just about make out what appeared to be blue writing across the chest.

'Oh God…' I said aloud as the penny dropped. I slowly reached for the microphone and pressed the button to synchronise with his cell, then paused for a few seconds, composing myself, wondering what to say. I was sure the steady hum of the tannoy was audible in his cell as it had been in mine. My voice wavered as I spoke a single word.

'Dad?'

CHAPTER 11

'Jimbo?' He stood in front of me, his eyes staring wide, waiting for my response, with the same crazy, wild-eyed expression on his face that he always had. 'Jimbo,' he repeated. 'Are you gonna help me or not?'

It didn't help that I was sitting on the floor and he was towering over me. I had one hand on my dog, the grey haired, soppy thing I'd named Sally. He had given her to me for my last birthday, one of the few nice things he had ever done for me.

He stood next to my uncle Robin, whom he turned to face before muttering something incoherent; I could just about make out something along the lines of 'useless kid'. He bent down so that his gaze was level with mine. He hadn't shaved for a while and his face looked grizzled and older. I could see the gap in the right side of his twisted mouth, where his tooth had been knocked out in a fight a few years earlier. The rest of his teeth had been ruined by years of neglect. His scruffy, light brown hair gleamed in the sunshine which poured through the lounge window. Robin looked at his feet, crossed his arms and used the carpet to clean something from his boot.

'Jimbo, it's very easy…' His expression changed, his voice took on a softer tone, and his nicotine breath puffed into my face. 'All I need you to do is to ride your bike outside the house I told you about. You just need to be my look-out, and block the road while we drive away. Do you think you can do that?'

I stared back at him.

'John, maybe he's too…' Robin started.

'Too what?' my dad snapped back at him. 'Too *what?*' he repeated, this time louder, and more threatening. 'It's not like I'm asking him to do anything illegal. He just rides his bike in the street like any other kid. What's hard about that?' His expression remained twisted with anger, and he rested his hand on Sally's head.

Seeing him touch something I cared so deeply about made me answer quietly, 'okay then.'

He softened. 'Good,' he said, standing up straight and looking at my uncle. They retreated to the kitchen, deep in conversation about the rest of their plan, details which I presumably did not need to know, although if I listened carefully, I knew I'd be able to make out every word.

I turned my attention back to Sally, who had now fallen asleep. I wondered why she wasn't intimidated by him as I was, and how easy it was for her to be so relaxed in this house. That's because I calm her, I told myself. I would probably have said yes to my dad even if he had not touched her, but I still knew he had done it as a silent threat: *say no to me and I get rid of your dog*. I would have said yes, because I craved his attention. He seemed so angry all the time. I blamed myself, though I hadn't ever confided this to anyone. Maybe if I were more like him, he'd like me more and want to spend more time with us, I frequently told myself. I couldn't fail to notice how little time he spent with his family. He never took us to the park to kick a football around, like my friends' fathers did. I knew we weren't rich, but kicking a football had nothing to do with money. He just didn't seem to want to. Too busy, too tired or too drunk.

I remembered seeing him out a number of years ago, standing outside a pub with his back to me as I rode my bike with my best friend, Chris. I recognised the grey hooded top before I heard his voice. He was laughing, in a way I had never seen him laugh at home. Luckily, Chris didn't recognise him; he was just another man who'd had too much to drink. Then I saw *her*, a woman who walked up to him and threw her arms around him. It was not my mother, and it didn't take a genius to notice that they were more than just friends. We rode away, and I edged slightly in front of Chris, partly to block his view and partly so he would not notice my cheeks, glowing and probably red with embarrassment and shame. Perhaps I should have spent more time with Chris over the years. He was very level-headed, and his normality was an escape from my horrible childhood. I could never confide in him, but sometimes just hanging around with him was enough.

We were ten years old that day I spotted my dad at the pub. After that, I began to mix with the wrong group. Chris joined in at first, hanging out at the park, but he drifted off when their antics got too close to the line; drinking and smoking didn't suit him. Maybe if I had stuck with him, my life could have taken a different path.

My dad's plan went well. Like a dutiful son, I rode my bike at the junction of the road as he'd asked me to. I didn't ask what he was doing or where he was. When he and Robin drove off, I did as I was told and blocked a harassed woman from driving off. I went home, some time before they arrived. They stumbled in, happy and already with cans of beer in their hands.

'Jimbo! There you are!' my dad greeted me, slurring his words. He put me in a headlock, slightly rougher than I would have liked. This was not an act of affection, more of a drunken embrace that you would give someone just as intoxicated.

'This, Robin, is my son. He will be my partner before too long.'

I smiled a crooked smile, and didn't point out that Robin was my uncle and had known me since birth. Robin reached over and ruffled my hair. They sat at the kitchen table, opening two more cans of cheap lager. My father beckoned me over, lighting a fresh cigarette.

'Come and join us, Jimbo.' He moved a seat out from the table with his foot. He motioned again for me to join him and placed one of the cans on the table in front of me. So I sipped the beer, which I choked on, causing them to erupt into laughter. I was twelve years old.

* * *

'Jimbo?' He stood up, his eyes staring wide, waiting for my response. His hair had looked unkempt the last time I saw him, but now he looked like someone who had been living rough for a very long time. This, twinned with a scraggly beard, reminded me of some kind of lost yeti. His face was dough-coloured and dirty.

'Is that you Jim? Please answer me, please speak again…' He trailed off, eyes wild. His voice sounded hoarse – through lack of use or constant shouting?

I had no idea what to say but I needed to say something, and soon. I pressed the button on the microphone again.

'It is me, but my voice won't sound the same…'

'No, I can hear it's you,' he replied.

I shook my head, confused. Maybe the sound-altering mechanism had been disabled.

'Jim, you've got to get me out of here, I've been in here so long, I haven't seen anyone for so long, I woke up in here…' He spoke ten to the dozen, his words a river of anguish.

My bottom lip trembled. Was this my future too? I

looked at his pathetic image on the screen. I had once been afraid of him, but couldn't help but pity him, once a strong man and now a shadow of his former self. Everything that had happened between us seemed to sink away, like the sand in an hourglass. I'm not like them, I told myself. I can see the good in everyone. I can't just leave him here. His grey hooded top was filthy, and hung off his frame. Cheese sandwiches and water sprang into my mind: the rows and rows of provisions I had seen.

He called my name again.

'Have you not seen anyone? What about *him*?' I asked.

'Him? Who do you mean? There's been no one. A tray appears through a hole in the wall and a voice used to come through a speaker, but that's it. I don't know who it is or where I am or why I'm here…'

'There's a man…' I said. 'Some kind of security guard, he works for someone I've never seen. This is some kind of prison.' My words came out rapidly, like a machine gun.

'Then you've got to get me out of here, find a way of getting me out. I'll die in here otherwise. I'll die Jim… *Jim*?'

I didn't know how to reply. I shook my head slowly, trying to think of something to say that would make sense. 'I don't know how,' I replied. 'I've searched, but there's no way in or out.' My thoughts drifted back to the fifteen screens, fifteen cells, fifteen ways in, but I had only seen one. Mine. Was this place all fake, an illusion?

'There's no one else here apart from us. Apart from some guy who murdered a girl…'

He paused for a while, then, 'Jim, *please*,' he begged. 'For God's sake, don't leave me in here. You've got to find a way out, please. I'm begging you, I'm your dad…'

'Okay, okay,' I answered, desperately trying to think if there was anything I had seen that could be of use.

Visions of boxes of cheese stacked on top of each other sprang into my mind but I dismissed this at once; they would never support his weight.

He went on, as if he was on a loop. But I was no longer listening, because silently, at the door, *he* stood. He could have been standing there for seconds, or for minutes; I had no way of knowing. Had he heard my conversation and waited quietly to see what I would do next? Was he enjoying witnessing what I had just discovered? A white gauze was amateurishly taped to his head, a small bloodstain emerging through it.

He spoke softly. 'And there sits Jim, and now he knows what this place is hiding…'

CHAPTER 12

His frame dominated the doorway, my escape route – not that I would have run past him anyway when I spotted the taser hanging from his belt. We looked at each other, frozen, to see who would make the first move. It was him. He grabbed at my sweatshirt so roughly that it bunched up around my neck, then yanked me effortlessly from the chair, flung me against the wall and pinned me painfully against it. He was taller than me, and tightened his hold, so that my feet were barely making contact with the floor. He slammed me back a couple of times, causing me to cry out in pain as my head made contact with the wall. My arms immobile and feet kicking wildly, the tears I had been holding in for so long began to flow. I was aware too of a damp feeling in my trousers, and something trickling down my leg.

As I writhed, embarrassed and in pain, he shoved me against the wall one more time, harder for effect, and then released his grip. I focused on the furious look in his eyes and didn't see his fist, which delivered a crushing blow to my stomach. I doubled over, aching, and sank slowly to the floor.

'Never feel that you have got the upper hand with me,' he spat angrily. 'I will make you one of *them*, and you'll wish I'd killed you.'

'*Them? Them?* This place is fake!' I screamed, everything I'd thought tumbling out of me. 'There is nothing here, I know everything! The cameras...' I gesticulated towards the screens. 'They're fake, I know they're taped recordings...'

He grinned at me, that evil smile. 'You believe what you want to believe Jim. But know that the Chief and I can lock you away so you'll never see daylight again.'

'The Chief? The Chief?' I looked at him with disgust. 'There is no Chief. *You* are the Chief!' I'd stopped crying now, and my breath came in dry heaves.

'There's just one bedroom here, I saw it.' I wiped my eyes with my sleeve, slightly more composed now. 'It's just you here. You're all by yourself...' I looked at him, waiting for some kind of reaction to this. I hadn't entertained these thoughts until now and they came out of my mouth in a rambling mess.

His face slowly broke into a smile and he crouched down so he was at my level. 'Oh, the Chief is real. This place is very real. You only have to look at your father to see that.' The screen showed my dad on his feet, facing the camera, shouting desperately into it, the sound muted. I propped myself up on one hand, the other clutching my stomach, to take a closer look, then sat down again on the floor, afraid to get up, my stomach and head still throbbing with pain.

'So now you have a decision to make Jim,' he said softly. 'Do you take the brown door or the grey door? Please think carefully and choose wisely.'

I stared at him. 'I don't understand... what door?' He motioned for me to sit back on the leather chair, turning it round to face me.

'Sit here and look at your father,' he instructed. I

assessed the threat in his tone and slowly rose to my feet. I hadn't noticed until now how much my ankle also throbbed, following my trip earlier. I didn't want to look at the screen, but there was no other option; I didn't want to look at *him* any more.

'Grey door,' he said. 'You came out of your cell through a grey door in the ceiling. Your father entered his cell through a similar grey door. One of your options is to join him, Jim.' He drummed his fingers against my dad's screen as if to emphasise this. He bent down to my level, close enough for me to smell his cheap aftershave. My eyes were wide, not fully understanding what he meant.

He sensed my confusion. 'You know you'll end up back here anyway. It's in your blood,' he whispered. 'Your father has made a career out of being a criminal; it's what you've been brought up with and all you know. What's the point in going home anyway? Your mother is practically a full-blown alcoholic, directionless, a steady flow of men through the door…'

'No,' I choked. I didn't want to hear any more. I had started crying again, tears silently coursing down my face in steady streams. This was a truth I didn't want to face.

'You'll end up back here,' he insisted. 'You won't be able to help yourself. I'm giving you the option to join your father in the same cell. Look at him Jim, begging for your forgiveness for years of neglect, for being a useless father. I'll even upgrade your cell, and you can live together, forging a new life. Grey door Jim. Choose this door and choose what is inevitable.'

Through blurred eyes, I looked at my father on the screen. He stood with his back to the wall, head in his hands, his posture indicating he was sobbing. Mr Greasy Hair was right, he had been a useless father. This pathetic figure in the cell wasn't the man I knew.

He snapped me out of my thoughts. 'Brown door Jim, is your exit from here. You'll go back to your home.'

He drew himself up to his full height and placed a hand on my shoulder. 'We both know what will happen though. Put a single foot wrong and we'll get you. You'll come back here, and I'll throw you straight into the well. No contact with anyone ever again until the day you die. You'll live without daylight, and go insane from the conditions.'

'Grey door, brown door, grey door, brown door...' He repeated this as some kind of chant. My head was swimming, my thoughts a whirlpool. I leant forward and slammed both elbows onto the desk, holding my head. I squeezed my eyes tight and covered my ears, wanting to block out as much as possible, and all the time he continued with his mantra.

His hand was no longer on my shoulder, but I didn't hear him fumbling for what was in his pocket. Two things happened at once: I suddenly heard myself scream, 'I don't want to go in the well!', then a split second later I felt a sharp stab in my arm before my consciousness ebbed away.

CHAPTER 13

A low whirring sound woke me from my sleep. My head felt heavy and my limbs ached, and I slowly opened my eyes and blinked in rapid succession to make sense of my surroundings. I lay spread-eagled, and a crisp, blue sky welcomed me, with wispy light clouds sparsely dotted round. I lay on dewy grass, which needed a cut but felt warm, making me think I had been lying in the same spot for a while. I rubbed my eyes, and made out an aeroplane gliding high above me. As I sat up, I swivelled around and saw a large tree, its branches gently swaying in the breeze as birds chirped quietly.

I rose shakily to my feet and stood up straight, but immediately felt dizzy, so I bent to rest my hands on my knees to stop myself from collapsing. Nausea rose from my stomach, and I stumbled to the tree, where I threw up violently until there was nothing left but dry retches. Composing myself, I drank in the clear air until the feeling subsided. Still using the tree as a crutch, I looked around. I was at the bottom of a large grass field, and in the distance were a few ramshackle farm buildings and a tractor ploughing a neighbouring field. That was where the humming was coming from. Behind me was what appeared to be an old, disused factory. Every now and again I faintly heard a vehicle passing, so I deduced that a road must be close by. I tested my ability to stand without support, and stood still, holding onto the tree until I felt able to move away without collapsing. With no idea where I was, I decided my most sensible option was to head in the direction of the road and possibly flag down a passing car. My ankle felt stiff as I limped through the long grass.

After a few steps, the horror of my experience began to dawn on me. I had escaped from *there*. Somehow I had managed to get out, but I had no idea how. I tried to recall the last conversation I'd had with *him*, and what piece of information I was missing, which had allowed me to get out of the room and into this field. I felt sick again, but this time with fear. Had I really been in there or had it been some horrible dream? The pain in my ankle served as a reminder that it was all true, and I lifted my hand to rub my upper right arm, which stung slightly.

I walked cautiously to the bottom of the field and spotted the road, a single, dusty track weaving through the fields. Climbing over a small fence, I glanced down at my trousers – they were filthy. I'm going to look a right state, I thought. That's if anyone sees me. I had no idea what time it was, or how long I'd been away. Last time I had been outside it had been late spring. I could be stumbling around early in the morning for all I knew.

The track led to a narrow tarmac road. Relief flooded through me; I wasn't in the middle of nowhere and should be able to find my way to the nearest town. I stumbled several times as I walked along the road; *they took my shoelaces*. No, not *they; him*. Some crazy man who aspired to be an Alcatraz-type warden, when in reality he was probably just a security guard in an insignificant warehouse.

I had been walking for about half an hour when

my surroundings began to become more populated. Small, sleepy cottages stood along the roadside and there were a few cars in the distance. I spotted a grey sign facing away from me, and ran towards it the best I could. It read 'Crenley Hampton'. I was on the edge of my town, though this wasn't an area I had visited often, for I lived at the far side, in poor town as I had often dubbed it. This part was very picturesque, and never in my wildest dreams could I have imagined living in a house here.

I had begun to shake slightly, from either lack of food or trauma, I wasn't sure which, but I didn't know if I had the strength to walk all the way to my house. But even if I did, then what? Would my mother be at home? Would she have been concerned about where I had been? I had no idea why the thought popped into my head, but I knew where I was heading. Sure, I hadn't seen him in years, but something told me to go to his house.

So I began my journey to my former best friend's house. Chris. He lived not far from me, but over the years we had lost touch. It didn't occur to me for one second that he could have moved away. Outside the front door, breathing deeply, I raised my hand to grasp the heavy knocker and rapped it sharply. After a few moments, I started to do it again, but stopped as I heard the faint rattle of a chain being unfastened.

'Jim?' It was Chris's mum, and her tone was genuinely concerning. She looked me up and down, eyes wide.

I stood with my hand leaning against the porch for support. 'I'm… I'm sorry,' I stuttered. 'I don't know where else…'

'What's happened? You look awful…' She reached out a hand. Thank goodness she had never been the type to judge me on my appearance. I was thankful that her first words hadn't been, 'Do you realise what time it is?' in an exasperated tone before shooing me on my way with a half-hearted promise of 'I'll tell Chris you called…'

I must have flinched slightly, but I welcomed her kindness, and before I knew it, I had half-fallen into her arms, sobbing. 'I'm sorry,' I choked as she led me into the house.

'Come in, you poor thing. Chris is still in bed, but you need to come and sit down.' I didn't want to imagine what I must have looked like for her to talk so gently.

Shaking, I sat on the sofa, hugging myself as I rocked back and forth. I fixed my gaze on the wall, from which light neutral striped wallpaper looked back at me.

'Let me get you a drink.' She quickly retreated to the kitchen, leaving me alone.

A figure appeared in the doorway, much taller since the last time I had seen him. 'Jim?' he asked, rubbing his eyes. He was dressed in a t-shirt and shorts; it looked as if my arrival had got him out of bed. I looked up at him, my eyes stinging and puffy.

'Jim knocked on the door a few minutes ago.' His mother came back into the room and held out glass of juice. I drank it, still staring at the wallpaper. 'Perhaps you could...?' she said to Chris, motioning towards me with her head. 'He's not said anything but...'

She left the room, and Chris closed the door and sat in a chair next to me.

'What's wrong?' he enquired, still a little groggy from sleep.

'I think I was kidnapped,' I said quietly, and began to pour out the horror of the last few days to him.

He let me talk, and sat there stunned as my voice trailed to a stop. 'You need to go to the police,' he urged.

I pressed my fingers against my temple. My memory was fuzzy. I had woken up in a field but couldn't be sure the distance I had been from the prison.

'I've got no idea how much of what he said was lies, and less idea how to track the place down. All I know for sure is that my dad is there. And no one, not even your worst enemy, deserves that treatment. I've got to get him out, Chris.'

He sat for a moment, considering what I'd said. 'If you don't know how to find the place again, then you must find the source. There must be a way for you to find him, this Chief. You say you think that you broke into his house?'

'*You*... you said 'you' as in *me*? You have to help me. I can't do this by myself,' I pleaded.

He nodded, accepting his role. Chris had always been the sensible one, and had a logical explanation for everything. 'Okay, I'll help you. So, this Chief's house?'

'It *was* his house. I know because of the picture I found in his room. But we're only looking for one person. I'm sure The Chief and Mr Greasy Hair are the same person...' I was mumbling now, not sure what to believe myself any more.

'Anything else? You need to think carefully Jim. Is there anything else you can think of that we could go on?'

'It's a large building with at least two floors. Very secure.' I tried hard to recall anything else about the facility I had been held in. The field I had woken up in had certainly not been close to such a building; there were only old barns in a state of disrepair. They must have dumped me in a random location nearby. 'Perhaps I should commit another crime...' I found myself smiling at my joke. 'Commit another crime and he'll soon find me again...'

'Hmm... I don't think so,' he dismissed me, shifting in his seat. 'If you say it was this Chief person, it's highly unlikely he will have the resources to watch you all the time. If it's just him, he hasn't got the manpower. It sounds like some cruel idea of a joke, just a sick individual who's got it in his head to punish you, for whatever reason. Maybe he'd been robbed one time too many. Then again, if you hadn't broken in to his house...' His voice trailed off.

I held my hands up. 'I know, I know it was stupid.

I don't even know why I did it. Really dumb thing to do, but I've learned my lesson.'

'Just a twisted individual's idea of a punishment,' he suggested. 'That's why you need to go to the police.' He paused. 'After you've thought of something to link him to what's happened. Think hard Jim.'

I breathed deeply, not wanting to dwell on what had happened, but at the same time desperate to think of something. I wasn't sure if Mr Greasy Hair had even told me his name. 'I went in his room,' I said, suddenly. 'There was a picture on his desk showing a fishing competition… from a newspaper, I think.' That was as far as my memory would allow. My thoughts had already started to fog and block out the surroundings, the smell… the isolation… the faces…

I put my hand to my head and rubbed my temple. 'I can't think of the headline… of the name of the town…'

Chris rose to his feet. 'I need something to eat, and you look like you need a shower and a sleep. Maybe things will be clearer after you've rested.' He was at the door by the time he'd finished speaking, so I followed him out of the room and upstairs.

'You can get yourself sorted in here.' He opened a door upstairs. 'It's Jen's room, she's at university. I'll get you some clothes…' He disappeared for a short while as I walked in and flopped on the bed, suddenly exhausted, the enormity of the situation rapidly catching up with me.

I had met his sister a couple of times and her room was simple with a feminine touch. I barely had the energy to take in the surroundings; even trying to do so seemed too exhausting, so instead I stared at the ceiling.

Chris came back with some of his clean clothes, neatly folded. My thoughts were swimming as fatigue overcame me.

I turned to face him, barely managing to mutter, 'Bakerfield's best catch,' before falling into a deep sleep.

CHAPTER 14

I was aware that I was dreaming but couldn't seem to wake myself up. I was back in the cell in this dream… *Why are you here?* ran on a loop through my mind. I closed my eyes again, desperately thinking of past events, which could link to my being imprisoned like this. I gasped as the face of a woman sprang from my memory.

***

It was a balmy Saturday night; my mother's birthday. My parents told my sisters and me that we were going to the local pub for a few drinks. Even though we would all be together, it wasn't a happy family gathering: more like, 'If you don't come, you can get dinner yourselves.' Since it seemed more appealing than spending time in our home, I decided to go. Any excuse for a drink, seemed to be my parents' philosophy. I had been out a few times with them, usually with the same excuse, someone's birthday, or my dad had 'come into a bit of money'. I knew what this kind of evening meant though: sit and watch one of them get embarrassingly drunk, or watch my father antagonise someone and pick a fight before I sloped off home, pretending not to be with either of them.

So I took up my usual spot, a few people I knew provided me with someone to talk to. The pub was fairly smart, with a seating area under a striped veranda outside. This was a space where people would congregate for a cigarette, often hunched around the patio heaters when the weather was cooler. But not today; as it was so mild, people were more spread out, and filled up the outside area. I was not legally able to drink, but my father always had more than one pint on the go, and didn't seem to notice I was helping to drink them. By now I was used to the taste of alcohol and I could drink with ease, not arousing any suspicion from the bar staff. I wondered whether they would challenge me anyway since I was with *him*, my dad. As he had a reputation of being trouble in the town, they would serve him cautiously and seemed to heave a sigh of relief when he decided to move on.

The pub was busy as usual. There was a party of women that I hadn't seen before, well dressed and not quite a fit with the usual crowd. I could just about make out their conversation over the music and other voices.

'Here's to Jill,' one said, raising her champagne glass. 'Who will be the best maid of honour ever...' They erupted into giggles as the woman who spoke lost her train of thought.

I looked at the woman called Jill. She was dressed casually but smartly and had perfectly styled hair, which she flicked with her hand. She seemed nice, much too old for me, but there was something about her that I was drawn to. Catching her gaze, I quickly averted my eyes, embarrassed. After a few minutes, I turned to face her again. She didn't see me this time; she was in deep discussion with the woman I presumed was the future bride. They were playfully teasing her about enjoying one last fling before settling down. I studied her for a few minutes longer, and her gaze momentarily drifted from the group, her eyes glazed over and her expression dropped, as if she were recalling a sad memory.

'Not much talent here though,' I heard one of them complain. This snapped Jill from her thoughts and she perked up again. 'Maybe we should move into another pub in town, somewhere a bit more...' They laughed in unison again.

Then I heard *his* voice. By now, my parents had migrated away from each other and were at opposite sides of the pub. My mother sat with her friends and my father had wandered off, bored, to see what else the night would offer him.

'Ladies, going so soon?' he slurred at them. For some unknown reason, my father seemed to appeal to women. God knows why, I told myself. He didn't really dress well, but tonight was scrubbed up the best he could. 'I can show you the best places you need to go,' he continued.

'Is there a nightclub in town?' one of them asked. *Don't talk to him*, I silently pleaded with them.

He squeezed onto the seat next to one of them, though there was not enough room. This caused a domino effect: each one moved slightly to accommodate the extra person. He snapped his fingers at the woman who had asked the question.

'The one opposite the bank?' They nodded and he smiled. 'There'll be a massive queue this time of night, but I know the owner. I can get us in to the members' room.'

He had got their attention now. I sighed to myself. How he could have the front to do this with my mother in the same pub? She didn't care though, he was out of her space and she could relax more. They seemed to exist like ships in the night, neither concerned with the other's actions any more.

'Do you really know the owner?' one woman asked, feigning suspicion.

'Do I look like I would lie to you? I have connections in this town.' He sidled closer.

'Jesus,' I heard myself say out loud. I'd had enough and turned my attention to my phone, randomly scrolling through messages: anything to not have to focus on his desperate flirting with anything female. *These women are too good for you*, I thought. I stood up, with the intention of going outside for some air and a cigarette. Of course my parents knew I smoked, but I still did it away from them.

I chatted outside to a few friends for about an hour before deciding to call it a night. I wanted to go home; I'd seen enough of my father embarrassing himself. Hopefully the group had seen sense and were long gone by now. My father would have moved onto trying to pull another woman, who would be unaware that she wouldn't be his first attempt that night. Outside the pub I pulled my jacket on, as it had turned a bit colder. Then I remembered my sisters. They were still quite young, and it wasn't fair to leave them here until my mother was ready to go home. I turned to head back into the pub and see if they wanted to walk back with me.

The entrance to the pub was empty. I quickly scanned inside, looking for them. As I was quite near the upstairs toilets, I decided to check there first before venturing in. I took the stairs two at a time, wanting to leave as soon as possible. As I headed towards the ladies', with the intention of waiting outside for a few minutes, out of the corner of my eye I saw them. A man, and Jill. She stood with her back to the wall, her eyes wide, searching. He stood against her, his body blocking her escape and gripping her wrist too tightly. I couldn't see his face as his head was burrowed into her neck. I regarded their clumsy embrace for a few seconds. Should I cough loudly a few times to disturb them? She did not look like she wanted to be there, and I had a sickening feeling I should distract him and allow her to get away.

Her glossy hair shone under the lights. Jill looked

fearfully at me, her eyes silently willing me to help. She squirmed like a fly caught in a web; she was his prey, awaiting her fate helplessly. Her blue eyes opened wide, pleading with me. Then it dawned on me: it was *him,* my father, with his latest conquest. I feared his retaliation when he realised it was me who had interrupted them. Coming upstairs was another couple, laughing together. With regret for Jill, I quickly headed back towards the stairs, colliding with the man.

'What's your problem?' he asked, aggressively.

I was halfway down the stairs when a woman rushed past me, hand to her mouth. I breathed a sigh of relief. She had got away from him; perhaps my own eagerness to get out had saved her. But I still felt guilty having not had the courage to do it myself.

***

I woke with a start. Chris sat with his laptop, frowning as he typed. He glanced up from the screen once he saw that I was awake.

'You were talking in your sleep. I can't find a Bakerfield.' He shook his head.

'What?' I asked, still groggy.

'You said 'Bakerfield' before you fell asleep. 'Bakerfield's best catch'. I thought it might be the name of a town?'

While I tried to make sense of this, he went on, 'I thought your Mr Greasy Hair might come from Bakerfield, assuming there is such a place...' His voice trailed off, almost embarrassed that he had reached a dead end so soon. I knew it was right up Chris's alley, exploring like this.

He typed slowly then quickened his pace, and his expression lit up. 'But I do find a Bakerfield fishing club.' He perched on the edge of the bed and turned the laptop so I could see it.

I propped myself up on one arm next to him to look at the screen. Bakerfield Fishing Club's homepage was displayed. 'Scroll down,' I said, 'there may be a news story or something.'

We saw it at the same time: a small picture of two men holding fish. I recognised them straight away; it had been the same picture I had seen in the room. 'Local men win with prize catches' read the simple text to the side of it.

'That's it, click on it,' I said quickly.

'Two keen fishermen landed first prize…' Chris read. I searched frantically through the featured story, eager for the information we needed. And there is was, innocently displayed in the second paragraph. My eyes, still blurry from sleep, had distorted the text.

Chris read it aloud. 'David Foster and Joseph Williamson… I think we've found him Jim.'

CHAPTER 15

I sat looking at my leg, propped up on a cushion. Chris's dad, a paramedic, had given me the once over. I had suffered no lasting physical damage, apart from a badly sprained ankle. He had frowned slightly at my agitated state when I had refused to reveal any further details of how I had injured myself. I had sworn Chris to secrecy, even to his parents, about what I had told him. We needed something concrete to go on and then we would be ready to go to the police.

'You'll need to rest it for a week or so,' his dad instructed me. 'Try not to put weight on it in case it goes again.' He paused for a moment, waiting for me to say something.

Chris broke the silence. 'Can he stay here for a few days while he recovers? His parents are away, didn't you say that Jim?'

I couldn't help but hear the sharp intake of breath. Chris's dad had heard rumours about my family, and had probably breathed a sigh of relief when his son and I had drifted apart.

'Just until...' Chris prompted him again.

'Okay.'

I couldn't help wondering whether the fact that I would be immobile for a while had influenced his decision. Had I been suffering from a broken arm, I was pretty sure I'd be out the door. Chris smiled at me as his father backed out of the room and closed the door behind him.

'So, I have a plan.' We were still in his sister's room, so he sat at her desk. I shifted slightly; reclining on her bed was the most comfortable I had felt in a long while. He pulled his chair over next to me. 'I've made a few notes,' he said, producing a notepad.

'We've got some names to go on. I'm guessing the names we found correspond to the men in the picture so...' He paused to check his notepad. 'Our guy is Joseph Williamson.'

'And the other one?' I asked.

'I haven't thought about him yet, he's probably just a member of the fishing club or something.' He waved dismissively. 'We'll look into him if we hit a wall with Joseph.' He brushed the hair from his eyes. 'I know, I know, I should be in the police force.' He smiled broadly at me, and I smiled back.

'You said he was a security guard?' He had written the name in the centre of a clean page, and started to draw lines away from it, constructing a spider graph.

'Possibly just a disguise. He may well be a security guard on the outside and go into the place still wearing his uniform, or he could just dress up like that to go along with the illusion.' I rambled on, 'but how can you be a security guard with nothing to guard? If there were no people in the cells...'

'You said there were definitely two though,' he reminded me. 'Your dad and the guy who killed the girl?'

My mind flashed back to my father's face on the monitor and his desperate pleas.

'Jim?'

'Yes,' I nodded. 'Maybe we should look into Emily's murder. I think he's her dad Chris. The guy is in there because he murdered her, but I'm not sure of my dad's involvement in all of this. And I was in there because...'

'He's targeting anyone who has harmed his family, do you think?' Before I had the chance to answer, he reached for his laptop. 'Then we start with her murder. We'll look into Emily's death.'

***

Emily leaned back in her chair. She sat alone in her bedroom, with no one to share the satisfied smile on her face. She was clever, but was never one to brag about it; she didn't want the look on her face to make others think she was looking down on them. She hovered the mouse over the Save button on her laptop, thinking: you may have well just got yourself an 'A' on this one. She thought of the letters on her desk offering her university places. If she achieved the top marks she'd been predicted, the choice of which place to accept would be hers.

Her phone vibrated silently and she picked it up to read the message. *Please tell me you are nearly ready.* She hesitated and typed her reply. *Very nearly. Just finished my essay.*

Almost instantly, her phone buzzed again. *I can't believe you are working on your birthday! And on the day you can actually drink legally too! I'll see you in half an hour or we might as well sign you up to the nunnery now! Xxx*

Emily let out a quiet giggle and closed her laptop. It had been an intense few months, and she'd struggled to get her coursework finished on time. She'd deliberately crammed in some twilight study sessions, keen to get finished before her birthday, the first big one, so she could go out and celebrate properly. She regarded herself as quite disciplined when it came to school work; this was just as well, as her parents were also advocates of 'work first, play later'.

She showered quickly and changed into the clothes she had already picked out. Emily glanced at her clock. Twenty minutes, not bad going. She checked her desk for her keys.

'Dad,' she called, and set off down the stairs. 'Dad, have you seen my keys?'

He looked at her over the top of his glasses. He was sitting at the dining room table, constructing a miniature model which required much patience and concentration. 'Your mum probably picked them up again. She'll be back soon.'

Emily looked at him. 'You're not going to say 'is that what you're going out in?', are you?' she smiled, mimicking his voice.

'Of course I'm not,' he laughed. 'You're eighteen now. But do be careful…'

'As always,' she muttered, going over to kiss him.

'I'm sure you'll be safely tucked up in bed when I get back,' he added, and she nodded. 'It's my last week on nights for a while, so we'll be a bit more organised next week.'

'Tell Mum to leave the door on the latch if she has my keys,' Emily said, heading towards the door. 'Love you!'

'Love you too,' her father replied, before turning back to his model. 'I'd better get ready to go myself,' he muttered. He didn't look up as his daughter closed the front door. Maybe he should have. It would be the last time he would ever see her alive.

***

The pub was busy and noisy as Emily stood at the bar with her best friends. She was the youngest of their group and finally felt like she could order at the bar with confidence.

If they ask me for I.D., I've finally got it, she told herself.

'Are we getting pitchers?' a friend shouted to her. Emily nodded, and turned to see a man staring at her. He smiled, and something about the way he fixed his gaze on her made her feel uncomfortable. He wasn't just looking, he was staring. He wore a plain white t-shirt and scruffy jeans. Despite the distance between them, she got the faint aroma of stale tobacco escaping from his clothes with every movement. Could have put a bit more effort into your outfit, she thought. He continued to stare at her and she smiled back awkwardly, and turned back to the bar: anything to avoid looking in his direction. He leaned in to talk to her, and she was relieved when her friend pulled her arm, drawing her out of the crowd around the bar.

'What a jerk,' she commented, too loudly; he stared, obviously having heard this. His gaze turned icy.

They settled at a table and whooped in delight as a friend placed two jugs in front of them. 'These are so expensive,' she complained. 'But there's an offer if you want to buy two at a time.'

Emily fumbled in her bag. 'I've forgotten my bank card,' she groaned. They shook their heads at her in protest. 'I can't let you guys pay for everything.'

'It's your birthday!' one of them pointed out.

'Seriously, I can't be without any money. I thought we were heading for a club later?' Her voice barely carried over the noise. She stood up to leave.

'There's no way you're walking home alone, not with all these perverts around!' Her best friend Sara began to get up to join her.

'I should be so lucky!' Emily replied. 'I'm only around the corner. It will take me ten minutes, maximum. It's still early and there are loads of people around. I'll stick to the main road, I promise.'

'Okay, but if you're more than fifteen minutes, we're sending out a search party!' Sara replied.

'I won't be long,' Emily called.

Outside, Emily pulled her jacket around her. She thought about her plans for the summer as she walked along the high street. Her house was only a few blocks away and she would be there in no time at all. People were still heading into town themselves so she didn't feel under any threat as she approached her road.

Her father's car had gone from the driveway. He had been working the night shift for the last month or so and she was glad he would finally be moving to days. She could see her mother had returned and left her car outside the house, leaving the drive clear for his return. Emily walked up the path at the side of the house; her parents often left the back door on the latch so she could get back in, though this time it was because her mum had taken her keys. She was known among her friends and family for being quite forgetful, so it had come to no surprise that she had forgotten something, again.

As she let herself in, she was surprised to see downstairs was empty. Maybe she's in the shower, she told herself. I'll just grab my card, shout hello and goodbye and get back to the pub. While there are still drinks on the table… Emily found her card under some papers on her desk. As she closed the door to her room, she could faintly hear talking in soft tones from her parents' bedroom. She frowned and walked closer, a sense of confusion washing over her. Maybe she is on the phone, she told herself; she always tried to think of a logical explanation for everything. She stood outside the door for a few minutes, her heart pounding, and was sickened to make out a man's voice.

Emily began to shake with adrenaline, and she willed herself to get out and not look back; but at the same time she was compelled to know exactly who was in the room with her mother. She leaned carefully against the wall; the bedroom door was slightly ajar, but not enough to look through.

'Jill, this is so hard for me,' the mystery man said

in a low voice.

'But I thought we agreed,' she replied soothingly, placating him. 'I'm not ready yet… Emily's about to sit her exams…'

When she heard her name, Emily shakily put her hand to the door. *This man knows me, or at least knows of me.* The door slowly opened, and she looked in horror at the sight before her. There were no excuses; certainly, 'we were just checking the bed for the loose spring' wouldn't cut it.

It was milliseconds before she heard her mother's voice. As if in a trance, Emily turned and ran swiftly back down the stairs, almost stumbling.

'Emily! For Christ's sake, Emily! Stop…' Her mother's voice was frantic.

The man was quicker than her mother. He had been able to throw some trousers on very quickly, and came chasing after her. 'Emily, stop, we need to talk,' he pleaded. 'Please Emily.' He caught her and held onto her arm, his grip too tight.

'Get off me!' she screamed, the tears already stinging her eyes. 'How could you? Just let me go!' The anger inside her mounted and she concentrated on struggling to get away from him, from the both of them. She pushed him, slightly harder than she intended, and watched as he fell clumsily into the metal railings at the side of the house, as if in slow motion. A protruding metal spike cut him as he tumbled face first, and she heard him cry out in pain. It was enough to stop his pursuit of her, and she briefly wondered if he had lost an eye as she ran down the street. I don't care, she thought defiantly.

Jo-Jo was what she had called him ever since she had learned to talk. Even when she was able to pronounce his name properly, the nickname still remained. Jo-Jo, the man she looked upon as her second dad, though they were not related in any way, was the man she had caught in her parents' bedroom with her mother. She ran, biting her lip to stop the angry tears from flowing.

As she approached the pub where she had left her friends, she slowed to a brisk walk. She hastily checked her reflection in the pub window and wiped her eyes carefully. I won't tell them, she told herself. It will ruin our evening. I'll phone Sara tomorrow and tell her the whole sorry story. She went back into the pub and forced a smile as she approached the table.

'There you are!' Sara stood and gave her a friendly hug. 'We were beginning to think you'd run off with the creepy man from the bar…'

Emily thought for a few moments, and remembered the man who had tried to talk to her earlier. It seemed like a million years ago, before anything had happened. 'Oh, *him.*' She wrinkled her nose in disgust.

She sat with her friends, feigning interest in the conversation, her insides churning constantly. Her mind replayed the scene she had witnessed, no matter how desperately she tried to forget the image and block it out. Just for tonight, she pleaded with her subconscious. Just for the next few hours, then I'll think about it.

The atmosphere buzzed around her, and people jostled past cheerfully. Emily felt her phone vibrate, and sensing it was *her,* she chose to ignore it at first. But the temptation to look at the message became too great. She held the phone under the table and scrolled through her messages.

Emily, God, I'm so sorry.

And within a minute, *please give me a call darling.*

I love you Emily, please call me.

The last message was only a minute ago: *Please let me give you a lift home. I'll be at Friar's Square, the usual place.* She shook her head and forcefully turned the phone off. Let her stew, she thought before reaching for her drink and downing it in one large gulp.

'Steady on!' Sara playfully scolded her. 'But it is your round…'

Emily winced as the full force of the alcohol took hold. 'No,' she said, 'let's move on to that club…'

***

Emily gripped the sink to steady herself. She looked in the mirror and was surprised to see how normal she looked, despite the anguish inside her. Her eyes looked heavy. She broke into laughter as Sara put an arm around her shoulder and began singing drunkenly in her ear.

'We'd better go…' Emily slurred. 'They'll be kicking us out soon…'

Sara loosened her grip and checked her watch, her wrist far too close to her face at first as she drunkenly misjudged it. 'And I'll be calling in sick to work in exactly… eight hours…' They stumbled together out of the toilets and found the rest of their party.

'Share a taxi…? There's a stand outside,' one of them said.

'No,' Emily put out her hand. 'My mum said she'd give me a lift home, she's probably waiting under the clock tower as we speak…' Outside the club, Emily could see her mother's white car in the distance, in the usual spot. She hugged Sara close, 'I'll call you in the morning,' she whispered.

A chorus of 'happy birthday' followed her, and she turned around, grinning and slowly walking backwards. Her expression morphed from cheerful to solemn as she slowly approached the car. What am I going to say to her? she thought. I'm not ready to hear her pathetic excuses yet. She turned around again and saw her friends heading towards the queue for the taxi. They disappeared into a crowd of people leaving the pubs and clubs the town. Her mother's car appeared and reappeared as she made her way through the maze of people shouting and laughing. As she's here, Emily thought, I'll walk home. That will give me a chance to think… She turned right sharply and headed back to the main road.

She hugged her bag close to her, not making eye contact with anyone. The air was fresh and she embraced it as it helped clear her head. Her mind was still fuzzy, with both alcohol and confusion, anger fermenting inside her once again. The crowds of people seemed to disperse until she was alone with the cars driving past. Emily reached into her bag, remembering her phone was turned off. *I wonder how many missed calls and messages I have?* As she pressed the power button, she lost her footing and the phone slid out of her hand and gracefully glided a few feet on the pavement in front of her. As she bent down to reach it, a pair of brown, tatty boots blocked her view. He managed to snatch her phone before she could.

Emily looked at him as he held it out to her, not close enough for her to reach out and take it from him. 'Thank you,' she muttered and put out her hand, but he didn't give it to her.

'Thank you,' she repeated, slightly louder. He grinned, sending an uneasy feeling through her. 'Or maybe not…' She tried to walk past him, no longer caring about her phone; she just wanted to get home.

'Don't you want your phone?' he taunted. She turned to face him and he held the phone out towards her. She hesitated and then went to take it. He grinned and laughed, retreating again.

'Whatever,' she muttered to herself and began to walk off.

'I saw you earlier,' he called after her. 'I saw you in the pub…'

That was when she recognised him: the man from the bar, the one she had dismissed at first sight. 'Not interested then and not interested now,' she replied, picking up her pace. Home was now her priority.

In a flash, a hand was clamped to her mouth from behind. She screamed into it, muffled, as she felt her feet lift from the pavement. Her body slammed against his; he had dragged her into an alleyway and stood with his back to a wall. Her eyes darted, desperately searching. She saw two other men circle them, menacingly mocking her as she urgently tried to commit to memory some clues to their identity. Her father was a chief inspector with the local police force, and had given her plenty of tips in case she ever found herself in trouble. *White t-shirt man and red and white checked shirt man and the man who has got me had a football top on,* she told herself. *One definitely has bad teeth, one missing...*

Emily frantically tried to recall the self-defence moves her father had shown her. With every ounce of strength she could muster, she managed to struggle out of the man's hold and forcefully shoved her elbow back. He moaned loudly and clutched his stomach. Her hair was painfully grabbed by red and white checked shirt man. He laughed, and clamped a hand roughly over her mouth, forcing it closed so she was unable to scream. From the corner of her eye she watched in horror now as the white t-shirt man slowly reached under his shirt.

Oh God, please no, she silently prayed, she feared that he was unbuckling his belt. Every move she made increased the other man's grip on her. Football top man had retreated to the entrance of the alleyway, still clutching his stomach, keeping a lookout.

'Hold her,' white t-shirt man snarled. He produced a silver knife, gleaming in the light from the street lamp. 'Hold her,' he repeated softly as he approached. 'I want to teach her a lesson...'

CHAPTER 16

'I don't see any story about an Emily Williamson,' Chris observed, scrolling through the results of a search engine.

'Maybe she had a different surname?' I offered. 'Her parents may not have been married.' It often surprised me that my own family all had the same surname.

'Hmm…' He mulled over this. 'Maybe I'll just look at recent murders in this town or nearby…' I edged closer so I was able to see the screen as well. The screen flashed up headlines to choose from.

'This is her, I think,' Chris pointed to show me. 'But it's Emily Foster…' He checked back to his notepad. 'He's not her dad Jim.'

'The other guy,' I urged frantically, 'Wasn't he called Foster? David Foster?'

Chris nodded and flicked back to the Bakerfield's best catch story. 'This guy is her dad then…' He penciled some notes onto his spider graph.

My thoughts drifted off. *The Chief is very real, this*

place is very real... The words hung like a speech bubble in the air. 'Maybe he is real then, and the Chief is not Mr Greasy Hair...' This came as no comfort. Sure, I had filled in a missing puzzle piece, but that just meant double the investigating, if we were tracking down two people.

'Joseph Williamson,' Chris interjected.

I nodded. 'He said he was Emily's godparent.' I was surprised how easily these details were coming back to me. 'What does it say about Emily then?' I was keen to fill in the blanks and find out as much as possible.

'Here.' He placed the laptop on my lap. 'You look, and I'll make notes.'

I clicked on the first story. Sure enough, there was a picture of the girl I now knew as Emily Foster. 'This story is a few years old. She disappeared on her way home from a night out. It says her body was found a few days later, throat cut.' It was grim reading and made me shudder. I scrolled down to find another story, something more recent. 'A guy was arrested but they couldn't find the murder weapon or tie him to the murder closely enough to convict... he had an alibi from someone who claimed to have been with him all night...'

Chris whistled through his teeth. 'Jeez, no wonder he was cheesed off enough to get you. You broke into his house and stole his daughter's picture, his *dead* daughter's picture...' He continued in the same vein, but I stopped listening.

'Chris!' I said loudly. 'I remember where this guy lives!'

I thought for a few moments and remembered the open window, the lock that had been so easy to pick, and the plush furnishings inside. 'It's very near my house,' I added, recalling my desperate escape from the scene of the crime.

I made as if to close down the laptop. 'No,' Chris said. 'See if there's anything else we need to know. Anything about Emily's parents.' He gestured for me to hand him the laptop.

I looked at his notepad and drummed my fingers against it impatiently, then watched as he typed into the laptop and swiped the mousepad.

'Christ,' he whispered to himself. He looked up at me. 'Her mum's dead too Jim. She drove her car into a river, not too long after the murder…' He shook his head. 'Something like that is bound to mess you up inside. No wonder her dad went crazy enough to set up his own prison…?'

I leaned back and put my hand to my forehead. It was as though all the pieces were finally starting to come together. 'I wonder how he got Joseph involved then,' I quietly mused.

'He was her godfather? Probably just as hacked off that justice wasn't done. We need to track them down and think what to do next.'

***

Chris's car was a modest hatchback. It had been reasonably tidy inside, his gym bag on the back seat, but now burger and chocolate wrappers were scattered on the floor. I sat, chewing slowly, watching all the time. We were parked opposite 23 Elm Avenue, the Chief's house, the house I had broken into. We had been here for approximately two hours, just watching and waiting. During this time, a man had passed walking a dog, the neighbour had taken in a delivery and a window cleaner had been up and down his ladder at several houses. But no one had entered or left number 23. I thought back to the old conservatory door, to the lock I had picked with relative ease. I was sure they must have changed this by now.

I broke the silence. 'Maybe I should look around the back?'

'No,' Chris said firmly. 'We are not trespassing on

his property. It's broad daylight and we'd probably be seen. We just can't risk it.'

Then why are we here? I thought.

He seemed to read my thoughts. 'We're just looking, there's no harm in that…'

'Look!' I said, excitedly, louder than I intended. We both looked towards the house, and sure enough, a man emerged. He quickly got into his car, frowning. I pulled my cap down over my eyes, in a small effort to conceal my identity. He didn't look our way though, or appear to know we were there at all.

I watched as he backed his car out and drove away, in the direction we were facing.

'Wait,' cautioned Chris. 'We can't follow him straight away.' He started the engine. 'Do you recognise him, have you seen him before Jim?'

'No but he looks like the guy in the picture.'

'Hmm,' Chris agreed, slowly pulling out of the parking space. 'I caught a good look at him. I think it's David Foster, from the fishing picture…'

'The Chief,' I finished. I sat upright and adjusted my cap, keen to keep my focus on the other car. 'Don't lose him,' I said, half to myself and half to Chris. A few streets later we hit town traffic, stop-start as we were approaching rush hour. Somehow this made things easier for us, made us less conspicuous and more able to blend in. I quickly wrote down his number, fearing we might lose him. He remained about five cars in front of us for quite a while.

'Maybe we could have found out more around his house. We could have asked a few neighbours about him…' I said. 'He might just be off to work or something.'

'No more breaking and entering!' Chris scolded, misinterpreting my comment as if it were my plan to break into the house again. 'It's not against the law to drive in the same direction as someone.' He turned to look at me, and his expression almost reminded me of a concerned father. 'Promise me Jim, that this is the start of a new you. No more breaking the law. You could end up in serious trouble.' After a pause he added, 'even more trouble than you were in.'

I nodded, exasperated. 'Okay, okay, I hear you.'

'You'll do more than hear me Jim. Remember, we are not breaking the law at the moment.'

I sighed impatiently as the traffic thinned and the pace began to pick up. We were driving out of town now and were three cars behind David Foster. The town disappeared behind us and the streets became less populated as we drove into the countryside. It was about half an hour later that David drove round a bend and disappeared.

'Where did he go?' I asked in disbelief. Chris remained calm, and he drove straight on. 'You need to turn around!' I said, looking back. 'He didn't come this far, we've lost him.'

'Relax, I'll turn around when I can. I can't just slam on the brakes. He's pulled in somewhere, we'll see more on our way back.'

Relieved, I spotted a road sign for a roundabout.

'Write this down Jim: we're in Brampton.'

We were able to drive much slower on the way back, with no cars behind us. The light was still good; it had been a clear, sunny day and sunset would not be for another good few hours.

'Here.' Chris pulled over. 'We'll pretend we've got a flat tyre or something,' he said, turning off the engine. He got out and walked round to the boot. I fumbled for the door handle and joined him. 'He went in there.' He pretended to rummage in the boot for something, but looked straight ahead, towards the entrance to a building that looked like a factory. Chris waited as a car zoomed past before running across the road. I followed his lead; he seemed to have a plan and know what he was doing. We peered through the heavy roadside bushes beside the entrance, and I could see David Foster's car in the distance, parked in front of a large farm building.

'So, shall we go in?' I asked, urging Chris to share his thinking.

'No.' He shook his head and turned as if to leave.

I remained in the same spot, 'But we've come all this way...'

'Then we come back another time. We know where he went, and we come back when his car is not here. There's a reason why he's here. There's something in there.' He pointed at the building. 'We'll have a proper look around when we're sure there's no one else around.'

CHAPTER 17

Joe dressed as quickly as he was able, pulling on his clothes clumsily with his free hand as the other pressed a large gauze against the side of his cheek. His face stung; he dared not look at it but the volume of blood told him it would probably need stitches. Beside him, Jill dressed rapidly too.

'I can't believe it.' She seemed to be muttering more to herself than to him. 'How stupid could we be? This is so close to the line Joe, so close. We have to stop, now.'

He watched as she tucked her blouse into the waistband of her skirt. 'Emily, my daughter, just walked in and saw us... and you're not worried?' she exclaimed. 'God knows what's going through her head right now...'

'How long do we have to go sneaking around like this anyway?' he replied.

'... and I can't bear to think what will happen if David finds out... like this. He'll kill me.'

'He'd kill me first.' Joe wasn't sure how true this was any more. David actually *could* kill him, but he served a purpose now. David wouldn't be able to run the prison by himself, as well as holding down his own job. On the other hand, he thought their affair had ended years ago, and that was part of the deal they had struck.

'How is it?' She carefully reached up to check his face. Her expression told him it did not look good. 'I think you need to get that seen to,' she muttered. 'I can't take you though. I've got to try and salvage this somehow.' She reached for her phone and scrolled through messages. She made a mental note to delete the ones to Joe, in case David saw her phone.

He watched as she typed a succession of texts.

'I'll arrange to meet Emily when she's ready to come home,' she explained.

'And what will you tell her?' Joe asked.

'I don't know.' She sighed heavily. 'I'll think of something.'

'Will you call me later?' he asked, concerned. He would have to head back to the prison straight after he'd been to the hospital. He sensed the night would be a long one and any communication from her would be welcome.

'I'll see what I can do,' she said. 'You need to leave now, while I straighten up around here…'

'I can help you,' he suggested. He really didn't want to leave her.

'No, just go, please Joe,' she asked, her voice heavy with frustration.

He couldn't think of an excuse to stay, and after a few moments. he grabbed his jacket and put it on as he walked down the stairs. The drive to the hospital was a short one, and he sat uncomfortably in the waiting room of the accident and emergency department alongside crying toddlers and patients the worse for wear after drunken nights out. I'll just tell the Chief I slipped down the stairs and went head first into the railing, he thought. It seemed a plausible explanation, as their building was quite old, and patches of rust adorned the metal work.

Fourteen stitches later he was back at his helm as if nothing had happened. He did a quick scan of the screens, physically and mentally tired, and with no energy to do a proper check of the prisoners. He made a note to see how the sickly man was holding up in the morning. With a heavy sigh, he lay down on the mattress in his small room and let his eyes close.

Joe was awoken abruptly some hours later. He squinted, unsure of the time as his room had no window. It took him a few moments to focus on his watch: 6.52am. He groaned as he sat up; it felt as if he had been in the same position since he had collapsed onto the bed only a few hours ago. He walked stiffly to the observation area, switched on the screens and held his breath. Sickly man was now lying down on his mattress. Joe studied him for a while, and he did not appear to move. The next screen to the left showed another man, on all fours, vomiting on the floor. Another man was in the middle of a coughing fit, silent heaves surging through his body.

Jesus, Joe thought, what is wrong with these people? A virus? Something in the water? Their meals were processed cheese and fresh bread, purposely chosen so there would be no risk of meat contamination. He shuddered slightly; he felt fine, but wondered if it was only a matter of time before he fell sick too.

He heard a door slam in the distance, the echo reverberating around the building.

The Chief strode into the room, looking like a madman. It was as if he hadn't slept, but was fuelled by a heavy dose of caffeine. His eyes scanned the room and fixed on Joe.

'You…' His tone was full of hatred.

Joe rose to stand in front of him. He wanted to be at his level for the inevitable confrontation. He shook his head slowly.

'You,' the Chief repeated. 'On this night, of all nights, I find out you have still been seeing my wife…'

Before Joe could answer the Chief flew towards him, pinning him to the wall. 'My daughter is missing… and I find out from my wife's phone that you have been texting her, meeting up with her!' he shouted, directly into his face.

'What are you going to do about it?' Joe managed to find the strength to argue. 'Are you going to kill me? Do it then, do us both a favour!'

'Kill you?' He slammed him back several times against the wall. 'Kill you? I am not a murderer!' Pinning him against the wall, he leaned closer, until their faces were almost touching. 'You'll beg me to kill you though…' He seized Joe's head into a headlock.

Joe sensed what was about to unravel and struggled as hard as he could as he was dragged out of the room, fighting hard to ensure the Chief's grip on him was as difficult as possible as he pulled him along the soulless corridors. They stopped outside one of the cells.

'You were like a brother to me!' The Chief spat. 'I treated you like family, and this is how you repay me!'

'It wasn't deliberate!' Joe shouted back. 'You make out as if I planned it all…' He found himself shoved against the wall again and released roughly, and he gasped for breath, hands on his knees. 'None of this was aimed at you,' he said quietly, between breaths.

He anticipated another punch as the Chief's hand sailed past him, but it never came. Instead, the door in the ceiling of the cell began to slide open. The Chief had pressed the button to activate it. Joe looked at it in disbelief.

'You'll beg me to kill you!' the Chief raged, and with one swift movement, he pushed Joe and watched triumphantly as he disappeared through the hole.

Joe landed awkwardly on the hard floor. It was only an eight-foot drop, and he narrowly avoided hitting his head on the floor. He turned, and with horror he saw a motionless figure on the mattress, staring at him, eyes wide open but seeing nothing.

With desperation, he turned over and faced the hole, hand outstretched. 'No, no, don't leave me here…' he pleaded. 'Don't leave me here with him!'

But the ceiling closed gradually and the outside slowly ebbed away.

***

He slept fitfully; for some reason, the lights had been left on. The air was thick with the stink of vomit, raw sewage and death. A pulse check had confirmed that the man who lay on the mattress was indeed dead. The man that they had referred to as Subject A – Steven Jones – was sprawled out in front of him. He had no idea how long the man had been dead, and he threw his jacket over him, in an attempt to conceal the body. But nothing he could do would disguise the smell, and the pungent odour made him sick a few times. He had no concept of time, but he was growing hungrier, and in need of a shower and shave. His mind drifted to Jill; she was by no means an innocent party in this. However, he didn't want to be the one to end things between them. Maybe it would be better if she was aware that her husband knew of their affair and then it would be her choice whether to continue. At the moment, it probably seemed to her that she was getting away with it.

As the hours ticked by, he began to worry that the Chief's plan was for him to die in the cell too. Though surely it was not in his nature to leave Joe there? He just needed to get his feelings out of his system, then he'd come back. He looked over at the body on the floor. He had wished the man dead, and there he was… but the fact was, it served as no comfort. It looked as if the Chief wanted him to suffer by having to look at a dead body until he could stand it no more…

A scraping sound startled him. With relief, he saw the hatch in the ceiling open and slowly grow larger.

Thank God, thank God, he thought. Whatever mood he was in, he was willing to talk about it now. Hunger was well established, and Joe was shaky as he stood up and faced the hatch.

No ladder.

He held his breath. Something wasn't right. Then an anguished face appeared at the top.

Joe squinted to focus on him properly. 'Chief?' he asked. 'David...?'

'I need your help. Things are very bad...' came the reply, in a voice heavy with fear.

Something was very wrong... Joe's first instinct was to run towards the hatch and plead for the ladder, but at that moment he feared the Chief's mood more than the prospect of spending more time in the cell.

'They are dying and I need your help... to decide... what to do...' The Chief crouched on one knee and looked down at Joe. He started to cry, and looked around, trying hard to formulate the words.

'My Emily... she's dead Joe...'

Joe shook his head in disbelief. He recalled she had disappeared on... that night, but he'd assumed she had run off in a teenage tantrum, angry at what she had seen. He had expected her to reappear later that night, have a tear-inducing argument, full of shouting and accusations with her mother, and crawl into bed, her head full of troubled thoughts before falling into a restless sleep. He'd assumed she would give her mother a wide berth for a few days, vowing to make her feel guilty and debating whether to tell her father about the affair. And Jill would have sat alone, worried about her next steps, debating whether to tell her husband the full story in her own words before Emily got there first. My version would be kinder, she would have told herself. I can edit out what I need to, and there will be no need for Emily to say anything.

Never did he imagine it would end up like this. Emily, his treasured god-daughter, dead. Was he partly responsible? Had she taken her own life, so troubled by what she had seen?

'How...?' He had to know, for his own sanity.

'Her throat was cut. I don't know what happened. There's no evidence of... any assault. No motive that can be seen...'

'Christ...' Joe ran his fingers through his hair. 'I'm so sorry...' he offered. He was about to say, 'I know how you're feeling', the standard response for situations like these. Ironically, he did know how it felt to lose a child in tragic circumstances, but he held back. He didn't want those feelings to surface again as they were still quite raw. The only saving grace was the macabre irony that the man responsible was lying in front of him: Subject A, Steven Jones, slowly decomposing.

'Rules,' the Chief began, wiping his eyes roughly with his hand. 'You must promise not to...'

'I'm not promising anything,' Joe replied, in a spontaneous moment of courage. 'We both know I could not promise that before; it is not just my choices you need to think about.'

The Chief seemed to ponder carefully on Joe's response. 'Then promise you'll help clear up this mess, the mess *you* helped make.' He moved backwards to grasp the heavy ladder, and carefully edged it into the opening.

Joe breathed a sigh of relief. One of the rungs wobbled as he put his weight on it, but he emerged from the hole, never more grateful for fresher air. He faced his friend, David, now broken himself.

'What do we need to do?' he asked.

'The prisoners... something is very wrong. Some more have died, some look ill, others are showing signs of...'

Joe thought for a moment. 'Contamination of some kind? Poisoning?'

David shook his head. 'I can't say for sure. All I can think of is the possible contamination from fertilizers nearby. We need to put together a plan for disposal of the bodies, and decide what to do with those who are sick…'

Joe nodded in agreement. 'First you need to agree we are equals in this. No more giving me orders. We will clean up this mess and make plans to move.'

'Move? You are looking to move all of the sick prisoners…?' David could not quite fathom what Joe was implying.

'No.' Joe began to explain. 'I think we can assume that all the prisoners are dying or will be dead soon. We are looking to relocate, set up a new prison, learn from our mistakes this time around to ensure that they don't happen again…'

'And then what?'

'Then I will help you, as you helped me.'

David looked at him, confused.

'I will help you bring justice to everyone concerned, for what happened to Emily. Let's say that if the judicial system doesn't get to them first or they don't learn their lesson, then we will make them see. And believe me, they'll beg us to end it for them.' He paused, studying David's reaction. 'Now, go and run me a bath and fix me something to eat. We've a long day ahead…'

***

David's experience in the police force meant he knew effective ways to dispose of bodies and remove all traces of evidence. All twelve of their captives now lay dead, and Emily added to this grim count. Thirteen deaths, they told themselves, but only one genuine loss.

'I've arranged for you to see a private doctor, to assess your health,' David told Joe. 'I need you declared fit and healthy if we are to decontaminate this place and… look for other suitable establishments.'.

'And you?' Joe enquired.

David sighed. 'I need to… be at home a bit more.

Jill is finding things hard, dealing with everything.' He found it hard to say her name in front of Joe; he had no idea whether they were still in contact. He dared not confront Jill, for fear of destabilising her any further. Her mood was already unpredictable.

'Help me,' David begged, a few nights later. 'Help me to make her happy again.' Ironically though, Joe could not bring himself to call her again. Was their last encounter their last ever? Would she blame him for Emily's flight from the house? Whatever happened, she would never look at him the same way again.

He would never know what was running through her mind as she drove her car into the river.

In the months that followed he and the Chief worked tirelessly, buying a new building in a new location. The old factory was now too much of a risk; all their previous inmates had died. In the new prison, Joe sat staring at Prisoner number two, John Hall, and silently cried at his loss. He and David were now connected in some way to fourteen deaths, and they had both lost everything that was precious to them. They were reunited in grief, with the sole aim of serving vengeance on all those responsible.

CHAPTER 18

Joe sat in the observation room of their new prison. He didn't like to dwell too long about what had happened at the old factory. This one was bigger, better, but the disaster of the first prison still gave him nightmares and he often sat bolt upright in bed, realising he had been dreaming. Despite this, he told himself that he had been the calmer of the two of them.

Now he sat in front of the desk in the comfortable black chair. The chair had cost a fair bit of money, but comfort was important to the job. He stared at the screen; the image had not changed since he had sat down. A pack of biscuits sat open beside a cup of coffee. It would be a long night, and he decided to keep his mug topped up.

He heard the door open and looked up.

'Joe.' The newcomer nodded an acknowledgement and removed his hat.

'You're a bit later than I expected. Any trouble?' Joe enquired.

David sat on the edge of the desk and shook his head. He rubbed his face with both hands, trying to wake himself up. 'Oh, just the usual at work. Mountain of paperwork…'

'Maybe you went back too soon,' Joe half-scolded him.

'I had to keep busy, otherwise my mind drifts and I end up…' he stopped, and wrapped his arms over his chest.

Joe nodded sympathetically.

'So, any change?' They both turned their attention to the screen.

'Nothing,' Joe replied. 'He's been the same since he arrived. He's not moved.'

'I must say, I'm not too happy about this location…'

Joe held up his hand. 'I know, it's not ideal, but…'

'It's too close…' the Chief interjected. 'Far too close to the town. People coming past might decide to have a look.'

'I'm working on it,' Joe replied. 'But don't worry, I'll deal with any trespassers. This will do until I can get things sorted again. We can't risk what happened last time…' He paused. 'So? Have you got an update for me?'

The Chief nodded. 'Let's go into the other room and I'll fill you in.'

They took one last look at the screen. The man lying down had had a heavy dose of sedative and would likely be unconscious for a while longer. That would give them plenty of time to talk.

They sat at opposite sides of the desk in the next room. These chairs were not as comfortable, but they would do. The Chief reached down and moved his holdall from underneath the desk.

'You shouldn't carry that with you everywhere.' Joe was almost scolding him.

'I'm not getting rid of it, if that's what you mean! This was a gift…' He trailed off as if he was recalling a poignant memory.

'I don't mean the bag. I mean what's inside it. The information inside it is very valuable to us. Everything is there, everything we've ever done, all the details of the inmates...'

The Chief shook his head. 'It goes everywhere with me and never leaves my sight. I'll fit a combination lock if that makes you happy, and look into what I can do to protect the contents from falling into unsafe hands. Fit it with one of those things that sprays dye on anyone who attempts to open it.'

Joe nodded. He trusted his friend, and had seen the bag safely in his possession for some time.

'So,' the Chief began, retrieving a file from the bag. 'Subject is a white 44-year-old male, called...' He rummaged through the file, which now lay on the desk. 'Hall, John Hall.'

'And he's our man?' Joe asked.

'Most definitely.'

Joe picked up his pen. 'Background?'

'He's married, three children, two girls and a boy. Eldest is James, he's sixteen, the girls are twins, Maisie and Gemma, they're fourteen. John has a long record of crime, he's done a few stretches in prison, theft mostly...'

'Apart from this one...' Joe commented dryly. 'His wife?'

'I don't think she'll miss him. Surveillance suggests that they've been living separate lives for a while now.'

'Any concerns with the children?' Joe looked up from his notes.

'Small world – the girls attended the same school as... Emily.' It was hard for him to say her name, the memories were still bitter. 'She used to mentor younger pupils when she started the sixth form. It's very possible their paths crossed.'

'And James?'

The Chief stroked his chin. 'We need to keep an eye on him Joe. He's been on the radar, minor brushes with the law.'

'Any connections with… our situation here?'

'No, none.' The Chief shook his head. 'James is not involved with any of this…'

After a few minutes, Joe spoke again. 'And how are you getting on with tracking down the other party in this?'

'The other alibi?' the Chief asked. 'Disappeared up north for a while after the trial. Believe me, I've got tabs on him.' He changed the subject. 'What do you have to report about our first prison? Did you manage to save anything?'

'The tapes,' Joe replied. 'I'll store them securely in case we ever need them. I managed to dispose of… everything else. Not easy when you've got twelve bodies to get rid of. The place isn't safe for us to return there.'

'That's good, that's good,' the Chief nodded. 'But we do need another prison like that one, more remote, though the underground cells here are ideal. This is too close to town, so has to be temporary until we can… relocate our guests…'

Joe was about to reply when faint sounds came from the adjoining room. 'I left the speaker on,' he said. They rose simultaneously and went into the room. This time the Chief sat in the black leather chair. John Hall, their latest captive, had begun to make low, incoherent noises, and was moving around slowly.

'It's a shame,' the Chief said, leaning closer to the screen. He spoke as if he was addressing the man directly. 'It's a shame that you're so close to the guy whose prison sentence you helped cut, but you have no idea.' He turned to face Joe. 'Since this is our second unit and the prisoners in the first unit were labelled A, B, C and so on… you can be prisoner number one. Our lovely Mr John Hall here is number two. And we've got the next cell ready for when our other alibi decides to come home.'

A voice interrupted him 'Hello?' He coughed

heavily, a smoker's cough, and asked again, louder this time. 'Hello, is anyone there?'

The Chief stared at him. John Hall sat up and pushed his grey hood back. The Chief pressed a button on the microphone to enable his transmission to be heard in the cell.

'Why are you here?' he asked.

They watched John look round, frantically searching for the source of the sound. His mouth moved soundlessly; the microphone was switched off.

'What's the point of asking him that?' Joe commented.

The Chief smiled. 'Just thought I'd try,' he replied. 'I don't care what his answer is.' He pushed back his chair and stood up. 'He's never going to see the light of day again,' he said dryly, and turned to leave. 'It makes no odds to me that he wasn't the one that pulled the knife on my Emily. He provided an alibi for her killer. As far as I'm concerned, he can rot in there.'

CHAPTER 19

David stood in the lounge, still trying to take in what was in front of him. The emergency locksmith was working on his back door. This was bad, potentially very bad, on top of an already devastating year. If bad things come in threes, surely this is me done, he thought. First the murder of his beloved only daughter Emily, then the suicide of his darling wife Jill; and now his house had been broken into. He felt numb, telling himself that he should feel more than this, but he was emotionally drained.

His phone vibrated in his pocket, disrupting his train of thought. It was a text from Joe, and it sounded urgent. *Come in as soon as you're up*, it read.

'One of the worst feelings in the world,' the locksmith commented.

'Hmm? What's that?' David murmured.

'Knowing someone's come in and gone through your stuff.' He stood in the doorway and looked around. 'Did they take much?' The look on his face said, *you've either been very lucky or had a chance to tidy up already*. David wasn't sure which was the case.

The man was looking at him, waiting for a response. 'Um, a few bits,' he muttered. 'More sentimental than anything.'

'That's the worst thing. Things that you can't replace. They need stringing up.'

David looked at him. 'They?' he asked.

'Kids. This doesn't look like a professional job. If you didn't have much taken he probably got scared. Mind you, I say 'he'. Could be anyone these days…'

David nodded, not really listening. The house seemed so empty and he hadn't summoned the courage yet to start going through his wife and daughter's things. It's too soon, he told himself. Emily's room had remained untouched since she… died, and his late wife's clothes were still in the wardrobe and her make-up and toiletries on the bathroom shelf. Some people had shared that they preferred to move everything as the constant reminder was too raw. David found the reminders reassuring; he wasn't ready to airbrush them out of his life just yet.

'Thank you,' he said as the locksmith started to pack away his tools. 'That was very quick.'

'You've contacted your insurance company, I take it?'

'Yes, it's all in hand.'

'And the police? I presume you've called already, as you've straightened things out a bit.'

David smiled wryly. 'I *am* the police.'

After a few more pleasantries, David shut the front door and picked up his car keys. He drove, slightly too fast through the town. The traffic began to thin as he wove through warehouse-lined streets, many occupied but apparently inactive; all the action was happening inside. Just like where I am heading, he told himself. He parked his car in the usual spot and headed out on foot, only pausing for a quick 360-degree check that he hadn't been followed or wasn't being watched by any workers on a cigarette break. All clear. He punched in the code and headed in through two doors and on to where Joe sat, facing the screens.

'Thank you ever so much for your call this morning,' Joe remarked dryly. 'I thought my days of being woken in the early hours were long gone.' He glanced at David, who looked agitated and preoccupied. 'What is it? And why the urgency with this one?' He nodded towards the figure on the screen, lying on the mattress.

David ran both hands through his hair, trying to shape his words into some kind of order. However this came out, it wasn't going to be good. There was no way he could sugar-coat what had happened.

'It's not good,' was all he could say. He puffed his cheeks in frustration. 'I've messed up royally.'

Joe cast his eyes to the screen and back. 'Why do I get the impression I'm not going to like what you're about to tell me?'

'Because you're not and you've every right to be furious.'

'Go on...'

David sighed again, and paced round the small room. 'I was woken in the night. You know I've had trouble sleeping since...' he said. Joe nodded.

'I went downstairs and listened behind the lounge door. I could've sworn I heard something, I don't know, a crash or something... At first, I thought it was the dog, but I froze for some reason.'

Joe nodded again. He had visions of David tossing and turning in his bed, desperate to sleep but unable to; he had done the same for many nights, and more frequently since Jill's death. He often resigned himself to the fact that he wasn't destined to sleep that night, and went to make a coffee. In a way, his duty at the facility gave him a reason to get up in the night. He found he could often nap in the day anyway, after he had finished all of his... duties.

'There was an intruder,' David went on. 'I got a

good look at him. He didn't see me looking through a crack in the door.'

'You didn't go and confront him then?'

David shook his head.

'I couldn't. I don't know why.'

'Jesus, did he take much?' Joe grimaced.

'A bit of cash I stupidly left lying around. An antique picture frame as well.' He paused. Joe knew which picture frame he was referring to, and what it contained. He had exactly the same picture of Emily on his desk in the room nearby.

'And this is the kid? He looks like a kid. You nabbed a kid for breaking into your house?' His voice rose in disbelief. 'Jesus, you can't just take anyone, let alone a child!'

'That's just the tip of the iceberg.' David looked at him, regret on his face. 'There's two very good reasons why I took him and when you hear those, you'll agree with me...'

'I'm on the edge of my seat.'

'He's John Hall's son.' He gestured at prisoner number two's screen. 'Do you remember, we flagged him up as a concern when we brought his dad here?' He pointed to the screen.

'I said he was one to watch and I was right. I thought he looked familiar even though it was dark. So I followed the little toad home, and he's living at the same address.'

'Okay, so you, we, were right to keep an eye on him,' Joe replied. 'But he's under eighteen, isn't he? I thought we agreed no one under eighteen.'

'I can't remember his exact age. He's around eighteen, he may already have turned eighteen since we brought his dad in here.'

'We don't need this kind of hassle. Just get him out. Check the file if you're not sure...'

'That's just it though. I can't...'

Joe cast a scornful look at him. 'You have got to be kidding me?'

'I can't check the file because he took the bag.'

Joe rose from the chair and shoved it hard. 'For Christ's sake!' he shouted. 'Have you any idea what this means?'

'Of course I have!'

'This is a serious breach of trust, not to mention a major lapse in security! How many times have I told you about that stupid bag!'

'And until now, it's never left my sight!' David shouted. 'It was a break-in; it's not as if I carelessly left it on the bus or something. Besides, it's locked, and the contents are…'

'The contents of that bag will bring us both down.' Joe spoke more calmly now. 'You and me on the wrong side of the bars. I don't care what you've done to the inside to protect the contents. If it's opened in a controlled way, the contents could remain readable. The point is it is now in the wrong hands. *His.*' He pointed towards James.

'His hands looked clean. No traces of dye and no smell of smoke. You can check when he wakes. He wouldn't have had the chance to open it.'

'And what do you propose we do with him?' Joe demanded. 'How exactly do I go about asking for the bag back without him getting suspicious? Why didn't you just grab it when you took him?'

'It was too dark, his mum was asleep, no other signs of anyone there but didn't he have siblings? I couldn't risk Mum waking up so I just took him. Before he had a chance to try and open the bag.'

They were both silent for a minute. 'So what shall we do with him?' Joe asked, calmer now. 'I doubt he'll talk to you over the loudspeaker, he'll probably clam up with fear. He'll have no clue where he is, and then we start droning on about a bag. Great plan.'

'Look, I've given him a stronger sedative than

usual. He will be out for a while. This will give us a bit of time to decide what to do. Ask him the question, give him something to eat and then bring him out of there…'

'Bring him out of there?' he echoed in surprise. 'We never let them see us!'

'This one is different. Give him the usual talk to scare him silly. We've done it before. Then let him go after he agrees to drop the bag off… I don't know where yet.'

'You don't want to keep him then? Even though he's John's son and we'll probably see him soon anyway?' Joe asked.

'No just give him a warning. It's worked well in plenty of other cases. Fit him with a tracking device if you want. It'll save us some time in the future anyway. Or arrange for Craig to collect the bag if you prefer.' David sighed, pleased that they had managed to talk through to a resolution.

'And from now on, the bag stays *here*,' he added. 'The only safe place there is from now on. Put it in the storage room when you get it back.'

They looked at James, still sleeping. He hadn't changed position.

'In the meantime,' David continued, 'I'll put together a file on him with the information we have at the moment. You can rig the tapes up if you want. Show him them, give him the talk and that should be enough. Once you've put the fear of God into him, say you want the bag back, to return it to its rightful owner.'

So that was the plan. Joe began putting it into action. He had no idea how James would react when he eventually woke up. He did look younger than his years, but considering his upbringing and the fact that he had just committed a burglary, anything could happen. Joe decided to take the taser with him, just in case. In the surveillance room, he arranged the recorded images of previous inmates to be transmitted on the screens; this is more effective than any lecture I could give, he thought.

He sat watching James for a while, thinking about how to bring up the subject of the bag. Ask in the wrong way and of course the lad would open it once he was released. The temptation would be too great. He would just have to imply that it was a present – which it was – and that was why he wanted it back. He typed a message on his mobile; a pity the reception was so poor here.

Craig, can we arrange to meet? I have a job for you. J.

Craig Tremell was one of their true success stories. He had stayed with them for a very brief period following a hit and run with him behind the wheel. He had known instantly what he had done and why he was being held in the cell. It had put the fear of God into him, and once he had been released, he had enrolled in college. Joe kept tabs on him; the tracker implant had worked well, and they had arranged a few meetings since. One of his uses was to observe other captives after their release, and report back. More importantly, he was also discreet and trustworthy: essential in this case.

He had one bar of signal on his phone: better than normal. Sometimes he had to resort to leaning out of the door or popping outside. He didn't like leaving the facility for long, and was wary about having his conversation overheard outside.

He watched as James began to stir on his mattress. The camera was also able to transmit night vision, since most of the time the lights were off in the cells. James went through the usual routine: reaching out aimlessly for any obstructions, moving towards the light like a moth to a flame. After a few moments, Joe illuminated the whole cell with the flick of a switch. I'll let him explore first, he thought, like they all do.

Joe cleared his throat and reached for the microphone. 'Why are you here?' he asked. There was no way James could recognise his voice; the distortion device gave it an almost chilling quality. A few seconds passed before the reply came: 'I… I don't understand? I'm just here, I woke up here. I don't know how I got here.'

'Hello?' the boy called. 'I don't know how I got here…' He raised his voice, agitated.

'Why are you here?' Joe repeated. Was it too soon to be asking him this? James might still be groggy after the sedative.

Joe's mobile vibrated. He decided to end the conversation with the inmate and stood up to answer the call.

'It's Craig,' said the voice on the other end. 'I'm calling you on a payphone rather than texting?'

Joe nodded. 'That's good. How are you doing?'

'All's good. I'm about to sit my exams, and I have a conditional offer if I get the grades. I'm still at the college for the time being but my university will be out of town…'

Joe already knew this. 'The best of luck to you, you'll do fine I'm sure. I've got a small job for you,' he explained. 'Our latest… recruit has stolen a bag from the Chief's house. I can't go into details; let's just say it needs to be returned as soon as possible. I'm going to question him about it, then arrange a meeting between the two of you, somewhere nice and friendly, so he can pass it to you.'

'Okay, that sounds do-able. I'll await your call.'

'Okay, I'll call again when I'm a bit clearer on timings. We can meet up so you'll know what he looks like.'

'Okay, that's sounds fine.'

'I'll be in touch.' Joe ended the call abruptly. It was time to go back to James and start the ball rolling. He quickly prepared a cheese sandwich and a drink; James would need energy for what they were about to undertake. Craig hadn't needed any further action than the question in his cell. This one was different; he needed to be shown what was happening; it was Joe's gut feeling that he would end up back here at some point in the future anyway. All he was doing was pre-empting the inevitable.

Joe decided it was worth the risk of getting him out

of the cell. Besides, he had to question him about the bag, and that would be difficult over the tannoy. At the entrance to the cell, he pressed the button and watched as the access hatch opened. James stood open-mouthed at the bottom.

'Stand back while I lower the ladder. The Chief wants me to show you something,' he instructed. The plan was to start with the talk about why he was there, then move on to the screens. Once James had safely climbed the ladder, Joe grasped his hand and inspected them for any signs of dye. Nothing. It appeared he hadn't had the chance to open the bag. David must have acted swiftly.

He led the boy to the small office adjoining the surveillance room, and decided to ignore James's obvious anxiety.

'Why are you here?' he asked again. James's expression suggested either he genuinely hadn't a clue, or was playing games.

Joe decided to rephrase the question. 'Why do you *think* you are here?'

James stuttered incoherently.

'Have you ever been in trouble? With the police, I mean?' Joe turned his attention to the folder David had prepared, and removed the paperweight from it. He hadn't had a chance to look at it thoroughly, and decided he would just have to read it on the spot. It contained David's address, since this had been the house that James had broken into. For a fleeting moment, he regretted reading the address out, but James's reaction told him it hadn't registered. The date of birth was missing; this was in the files in the bag.

'How old are you? The file doesn't say.' He cast his eyes up and down the boy. David had remembered his physical description well. His mousey brown hair was tousled and he wondered whether it was always as unkept or if that was because of the situation.

'Nearly eighteen,' came the reply.

'I didn't think we were taking them that young…' Joe mused. They had decided that eighteen was the minimum age of the prisoners they would have. He recalled a conversation he'd had with David. 'Whatever we're doing here,' he'd explained, 'I can't justify taking anyone underage. I mean, God forbid if this ever got out, not that it will, I can't add child abduction to the mix.'

Joe tried to clear his thoughts, this was information he would not be sharing with James.

As the conversation progressed, Joe found he was getting through to James, who appeared genuinely scared. Time to play my trump card, thought Joe. Show him the room. He'll be too shocked to notice they are tapes; he'll only give them a glance, and he'll be too shocked to pay much attention.

He watched as James stared at the screens in disbelief. It was working. He was too dumbstruck even to register that the figure on one of the screens was his father, who had been missing for about a year. For some reason, Joe felt the need to tell him about Emily and her murderer. He would be one of the few people who would learn the main reason the facility existed. He hadn't really spoken to anyone about everything that had happened. He had considered therapy afterwards, but didn't feel ready to talk to anyone about it then. He poured out the background to James and found it was still painful. He closed his eyes to compose himself; hold yourself together, he told himself. This is not the time or place to crumble. You're going off track… the bag, don't forget the bag…

And then there was physical pain to accompany the internal torture. Joe opened his eyes slowly to try and comprehend what had just happened. He lay slumped back in the chair, and a dull ache clouded his vision. It took him a few moments to remember where he was. *Did I faint? Did I black out and hit my head?* He looked to the floor and saw the glass paperweight nestled against the skirting board. Anger welled up inside him.

They had seriously underestimated James Hall. He gritted his teeth, and decided to go to the storage room. It was locked, so James had no chance of getting inside if he was poking his nose around the facility, which Joe was sure he was doing right now. He's trying to find a way out, he thought. But all he would see was Joe's own room and the kitchen, and there was nothing incriminating in there. Knocking several things over in frustration, he rifled through the medical supplies for something to stem the flow of blood to his head. A quick wipe had told him it wasn't too serious.

He rapidly scrolled through the contacts on his phone.

'Chief? It's me,'

'Joe? Is everything okay?' His voice was muffled and the line crackled.

'Things aren't going to plan here. James attacked me, threw a paperweight at me... hit me on the head, knocked me out cold...'

'He... what? Are you okay?'

'I'm fine, but he's somewhere on the ground floor, I don't know where...'

'You don't know where he is?' The Chief's voice grew clearer. 'Find him!'

'Don't worry, he can't go anywhere. I still have the keys, he wasn't clever enough to take them. Probably just ran out of the room, looking for a door...'

'Okay.' He sounded calmer now. 'How do you want to proceed?'

'I haven't even asked him about the bag yet.' A heavy sigh came down the phone line. 'But I want him out of here.' Joe spoke firmly. 'He'll probably go to the police, to you anyway. You'd better make sure you're ready for him...'

After a pause, Joe heard David speak, 'fine, fine. You contact Craig and have him follow him to see what he does.'

The line went silent.

***

David mulled over the situation. Paperwork was stacked haphazardly on the right of his desk. The stack on the left was markedly smaller. This meant he was in for several late nights in the next few weeks. He threw a glance through his door to the open plan office, where his colleagues busied themselves. The member of staff he needed to talk to became available and he seized his opportunity.

'Simon, a word?' he called from the office door. A slightly overweight officer headed towards him.

'There's something I need to talk to you about,' he said as they both sat down. Simon gave a quick nod.

'I am anticipating that a young man may call in the station soon and I want you at the front desk to deal with him.'

Simon began to rub his temple, obviously troubled. 'And this young man, what will he ask?'

'He's going to tell you a story about being held prisoner. He will implicate Joe, and give you details of other people being held captive. I want you to listen, then refer him to me, while he is still on the premises. And please don't discuss this case with anyone else…'

'Jesus, David, I can't keep doing this for you… What you're doing…'

David gazed calmly at his colleague. He turned over a fountain pen with his fingers like a majorette's baton. Inwardly, his patience was thinning.

'And tell me Simon, how is the McGinty case proceeding? The evidence you *found,* did that move the suspicion away from the suspect? And I'm sure you haven't had anything to do with the hush money that was used to get him off the hook…'

Simon held up his hand. 'Okay, okay…'.

David moved closer to the desk and pressed his palms on the surface. 'Don't you dare for one second question my authority. I have turned many a blind eye to your dealings…' He paused to rein in his irritation.

'Know that what I'm doing, Simon, is worthy, and beneficial to everyone.' He was calmer now, and spoke more quietly. 'Not just to us, here at the station, but everyone out there.' He watched Simon's expression change and his gaze drop towards his shoes.

'This young man, then… what's his name?'

'James Hall. Or he may call himself Jim.'

He watched as Simon nodded. Stupid, incompetent idiot, David smiled to himself. Useless at his job, PC Simon Fowler seemed to spend most of his time at the vending machine. Sooner I can get rid of him, the better. But the truth was at this moment, he needed him. Simon was easy to control and the mere threat of ratting him out due to his own seedy activities only seemed to scare him further.

* * *

Simon sank back into his chair, still simmering at the dressing down he had just been given from his boss. He hated himself for being intimidated so easily. But he had gotten himself backed into a corner that was too difficult to get out of. An innocent gambling habit had quickly spiralled out of control. At first it had just been a few visits to the local casino to rid himself of the endless nagging from his wife at home. Then he found he was returning in a desperate attempt to clear himself of the mess he now found himself in. His debts were now increasing, a yawning hole into his overdraft and soon he was struggling to make minimum payments.

He had blurted some of this out to David on one occasion. The weight he carried on his shoulders momentarily lifted before pressing back down, almost crushing him. David hadn't appeared shocked in hearing the situation he was in.

'You need a loan, is that what you are asking me?' David had questioned him.

Simon shuffled from foot to foot. 'I'm due some money in any day now. Mother-in-law pegged it a few months ago and the inheritance is coming through soon.' The lies came easily to him.

Without a word, he watched as David reached into his drawer and placed out two bundles of cash in front of him. He pushed it temptingly closer.

'You're sure?' he smiled widely, relieved. This was all he needed as he was sure tonight his luck would change. A gambler was due a massive win at some point and this would be his chance. Bet on the right numbers and things would be on the up.

'Take it,' David had reassured him.

He reached for it greedily, more desperately than he wanted his boss to see. He ran his fingers over the edges of the bank notes. Had David not have been in the room, he would have raised them to his nose and inhaled their dizzy aroma.

In less than five hours, he had lost the lot. Although this had not been before he had actually doubled his money but his addiction was now too controlling that he had been too blind to see this and walk away.

David noticed the stress that must have been etched on his face. 'Home life still tough, eh?'

Simon shook his head slowly, 'damn solicitors… dragging their heels…' He added another brick to his wall of lies. He swallowed hard and ran his palms over his trousers to dry his now sweaty hands. He was sat opposite David, the desk between them. Thankfully his boss could not see his trembling legs.

'I might be able to help you,' David announced as he opened his desk drawer.   He positioned two more bundles of cash between them. He watched as Simon's eyes lit up and his hand jutted out to snatch it.

This time though, he kept his hand over the money and pulled it back a few inches towards him. Simon's hand hovered mid-air before slowly retreating, an animal backing down in a fight.

'This time, I want a favour from you,' he began to explain quietly but clearly. 'Close my door please.'

Simon obeyed before sitting himself back down, intrigued.

'I want you to meet me at this address tonight,' he pulled a folded note from his jacket pocket. 'I need your help with something…'

'Okay…' he heard himself agree, so desperate for the cash and without any idea what he was agreeing to.

'Should everything go to plan, the money will be yours.'

Later that evening, Simon sat in a dimly lit housing estate. It was late, not that this was a problem for him as usually at this time of night, he was sat in a casino bar weighing up his losses. He checked the address several times, wondering what he was doing there. For a fleeting moment, he worried he was at the wrong location. The minutes ticked by slowly as the car engine idled quietly. In the distance, he saw the black outline of a figure raising his hand – the signal he had been waiting for. Quickly, he cut the engine and scrambled out of the car towards him.

David's hat masked the top half of his face and the hood from his jacket was pulled up. Despite the darkness, he wore sunglasses and Simon could see his distorted reflection in these. He gestured for Simon to follow him inside the house. Carefully, David's gloved hands opened the back door.

Simon squinted in the darkened room as they lost the moonlight. A body lay sprawled out on the sofa in front of them.

'Is he…'

David shook his head, 'no, just unconscious, that's

all,' he shuffled in his pocket, appearing to conceal the reason why the person lay unresponsive. 'I want him in the car. You will take one of his arms for us to support him. Make it look as though he is walking out…'

He grunted as he hoisted the stranger up, David taking the other side. The weight indicated it was a man they were moving. He wanted to ask who it was, what he had done and where he was being taken to. But he kept his mouth shut, the promise of the cash a domineering thought in his head.

David took the wheel and drove away. Simon waited for an explanation of what he had just helped with but none came. He didn't pay particular attention to where David was driving to but after a while, he pulled over.

'Glove box…'

He sat confused and heard David sigh quietly. He reached over and pulled the catch so the cover sprang open. The light glowed around the wads inside.

'Take them, they are yours…' David indicated to him. 'And now, I'd like you to get out,' he stated.

Simon's jaw dropped of its own accord. He was in the middle of nowhere, not recognising his surroundings. He stuttered a few words and then reached for the door handle. He looked back at his boss, now even more of a mystery to him.

David reached for the handle on the inside, 'you are to discuss with no one what you saw tonight. I may need your help again at some point and I do not want any questions, do you understand?' He watched as Simon nodded dutifully.

'I will make it worth your while,' he added before pulling the door to him signaling that Simon should not have any questions about tonight.

It wasn't long before Simon began to rely on these encounters as a way of keeping himself from treading water financially rather than almost drowning. The slow drip feeding of David's cash became a crutch of support. He wasn't a stupid man, of course he knew whatever David was involved in was illegal and he had now become an accomplice in this. Moving bodies in the dead of night? Even if they were only unconscious and not dead didn't change anything. His conscience got the better of him at one point but David's withdrawal of cash left him gasping for air.

He hadn't kept an accurate tally but reckoned he'd been associated in helping shift at least ten different men. For some reason, they were all men. After a while, David had put him on the McGinty case and soon he was able to take bribes to keep the accused out of prison. He had found himself planting fake evidence to shift the blame and was rewarded with a large sum – but not before David had taken back his share.

'I want no more to do with it,' he had protested one night. 'Whatever you and Joe are into, I'm out.'

David had moved to him at once and had him cornered in his office. He didn't even need to lay a finger on him, his chilling glare routed Simon to the spot almost instantaneously. His back pressed against the wall, clearly overpowered.

'Out?' he glared at him. 'Out?' he repeated himself. 'There is no out for you. I can destroy you. You will lose everything. House, job, family, all gone,' he waved his hand in a sweeping motion.

Simon broke his wide-eyed gaze first. He stared at a spot on the opposite wall, a stabbing pain coursed through his stomach. He was well and truly trapped under this man's spell. The only way out that he could see was for one of them to die. The true coward that he had now become told him that there was no way it would be him.

CHAPTER 20

Within the month, David met up with Joe again, this time in his office. It was the end of the day, and only a few people remained in the main office. Joe had waited patiently for his friend to become free, not before he had given a colleague a severe telling off.

David had closed the door giving them privacy. 'The idiots I have to work with,' he sighed. 'I've downloaded James's activity from the tracker,' he changed the subject. 'You dropped him off here, right?' He pointed to a location on the map on his laptop screen.

Joe squinted at the screen. 'That looks about right, on the edge of town.'

'Looks as though he's stayed in town except for one trip out, to a point close to the river. I can only assume it's our fishing club?'

'Persistent, isn't he?' Joe observed. 'What does he think he's going to uncover there?'

'Who knows? He's probably just investigating. He's also spent some time here.' He indicated a residential area on the map. 'My neighbourhood. So this is what I think we should do. I'm going to lead him to the old factory…'

'That's close to where he was dropped off!' Joe exclaimed. 'That's a bit risky…'

'I very much doubt he'll put two and two together. He was probably too out of it to take in his surroundings when he woke up. I presume you put him near the road?' David didn't wait for an answer. 'I'll lead him to the other side of the factory, and we'll trap him in there somehow.'

'You think he'll go in?'

David paused for a second. 'I do. And we'll lay a bait. If we move his dad there for a while, he'll believe that was where he was held. I'll wait nearby and follow him in, or wait for him to call the police so I'll be dispatched there. I can sort something out from there.'

* * *

I sat on my bed, impatiently fidgeting and trying to plan my next move, obsessed with finding out more about the factory that we had been led to. I was back at my own house now; my ankle was almost better, and I could pretty much walk normally. When I left Chris's house, I made a big show of thanking his parents, letting them know how grateful I was.

Next to me on the bed were the notes Chris and I had made. I still had the picture of Emily, and the watch and leather bag. I figured the bag weighed about four kilos, but shaking it gave no indication what was inside. Paperwork for his job probably. I ran my fingers over the lock, wondering how I could break into it, but I remembered Chris's insistence on playing the model citizen. I didn't think I could ever pass for a model citizen, but the bag might well be worth more to me if I did not tamper with it. I shoved it to the floor and used my foot to push it under the bed. Chris insisted we weren't ready to make a move yet, that we needed more information about the place David Foster drove to so regularly. We had followed him a few more times, and a pattern was emerging; he seemed to leave at the same time every few days, always in a hurry, always looking confused.

We had driven to the fishing club one afternoon, but something had prevented me from going into the clubhouse. Instead, we sat in their car park, me jittery and anxious, and Chris wondering why he had agreed to go in the first place.

'What were you expecting us to uncover here?' he had asked with a hint of annoyance.

'I don't know,' I confessed. 'Something, anything about them. How often they come here, if they still come at all now they are so busy…'

'And you really thought the leader of the club, or whatever he's called, would happily give us all this information?' He was mocking me. 'Oh yes,' he continued in a comical voice. 'David and Joseph were just here the other week. They fish here quite regularly. Their addresses? Why of course…'

'Okay, okay! Stupid idea. Let's just go, then.'

'Maybe it's time to look in the old factory building,' I proposed one Saturday in town. 'We know when David is there; we can go when he isn't.' I got the feeling he wasn't really listening. 'Every day my dad stays in there…'

He stopped to look at a news stand, 'Human remains in grim discovery' announced a headline. 'That's not all that far from here,' Chris remarked, scanning the article. We didn't talk about this any further, the subject went out of my mind.

We went into a sports shop and Chris began idly browsing through the display racks. I did not feel comfortable outdoors yet and was constantly looking over my shoulder. Crowded places worried me, but when I was alone memories haunted and taunted me. We had passed a coffee shop earlier, and I did a double-take, convinced *he* was there, at a table, sipping his drink.

I stood near Chris, feeling edgy and twitchy. His casual take on all this annoyed me at times.

He looked at me. 'Okay, maybe you're right. Maybe we should go back to the factory. But it will have to be tonight. It's not one of his usual days.'

I smiled in relief. 'Let's go back home and talk through the plan then.'

Chris left the shop first and I let a couple of giggling girls go ahead of me. I knew that they were probably looking at him, not me. As I left an alarm sounded sharply, and for a moment I panicked as the security guard approached me. But my shopping bag had a receipt inside, and for once I had nothing to fear. A guilty conscience after my past trips to the shopping mall made me nervous.

Chris was waiting for me. I shrugged at him and mouthed, 'I don't know…?'

The security guard motioned for me to go back into the shop. His uniform sent chills down my spine. He glanced in my bag briefly, and finding nothing, he handed it back.

'Am I free to go?' I asked. He nodded. I walked through the barrier again – and the same thing happened, then again a third time.

'Here.' I handed my bag to Chris and with nothing in my hands, I went to pass through the security barrier for what I hoped was the last time. The same noise resonated.

'Odd,' commented the guard. 'Sometimes it's something in your clothes…' He waved me out, dismissively. I'm sure it's the metal zip in my jacket, I told myself, without quite believing it. People stared as we walked towards the exit, but we soon blended into the crowd.

Chris smiled. 'A friend of mine once sewed a piece

of metal into his brother's coat, and every time he went through one of those things, he set it off,' he said. 'Really cheesed him off, it did.' He didn't seem to think it odd that I had set off the alarm, and I was relieved as he didn't ask about it. 'So?' he asked. 'Back to yours?'

***

Later that evening we parked on the edge of town and decided to make the rest of the journey on foot. We suspected we were about to stumble on their secret base, but had not discussed what we might find there.

At first, Chris talked about his eighteenth birthday party, the girl he'd met there that he planned to ask out and how he was going to travel around Europe in the summer holidays. I pretended to listen, but I was preoccupied, anxious about what we might find. I had not made any plans, and in the pub a few nights earlier I had chatted to a few girls but made polite excuses to leave. Small talk seemed difficult for me at the moment.

'Maybe I should've looked in the bag,' I muttered.

'What bag?'

'When I… broke into his house, I took a bag…'

'And you didn't look in it?' he interrupted. 'It could have been important. More evidence.'

'But… but… it was locked,' I replied, but it sounded pathetic even to me. I had been taking his advice, trying to do the right thing, and here was Chris, suggesting I rifle through the Chief's possessions. 'I'll do it when we get back,' I decided.

'We need as much evidence as possible,' he reminded me.

We walked through the field next to the road. The factory building loomed in the distance. 'I think the coast is clear,' I said. No vehicles were outside, just the tall factory, ominously ahead of us.

Chris looked around the front of the building. 'I

don't see any security cameras,' he said. It was made up of corrugated metal panels and grey, shabby brickwork overgrown with tufts of grass around the perimeter. It looked familiar, but I couldn't figure out why.

A small flight of metal steps led up to a small door, and I could see a large silver padlock on it. I drew Chris's attention to it. 'I think that's out of the question.' I carefully climbed the steps to take a closer look; the lock looked almost brand new and lay heavy in my hand. It was a combination lock, and the barrels moved smoothly. I turned to face Chris, shook my head and went back to join him.

'Okay, let's see if there's another way in.' he said. We walked around to the back of the building. There were only fields behind, and the road was just a murmur in the distance. Sure enough, there was a plain white door. It looked as though someone was in the process of fitting a security bar on it.

'Are you sure about this?' Chris asked. My heart in my mouth, I nodded.

He breathed deeply, 'Okay then, let's do this.'

The door opened easily.

The first thing to hit me inside was the darkness, and how warm the air felt. I blinked several times to get my eyes used to the change from bright light to none at all. Chris felt around on the wall, looking for a switch. In true Hollywood style, I walked ahead and lit a few matches, wincing as the flame burned close to my fingers.

'Found it!' exclaimed Chris. A series of small lights buzzed on from the walls. I swallowed hard. Suddenly this was all too familiar, and for a moment I wished we weren't here.

'Chris, wait…' I stopped in my tracks, afraid. 'Maybe this isn't a good idea…' But he walked carefully along the corridor, beckoning me to follow, fascinated by what was ahead.

'Ssshhh,' he whispered, 'I think I can see

something.'

I followed reluctantly, then I saw it too. On the ground ahead was a metal grille. My heart began to race. 'God, I've seen this before,' I panted, falling to my knees next to Chris. 'I know what it is…' He looked at me, willing me to go on. 'It's where they pass you the food.' I bent down, my ear touching the ground, eager to see in as far as I could. Chris made a half-hearted attempt to open the grille.

'No,' I said, 'there's a button which releases the catch.' I pressed it and heard an audible click. I prised the grille open and motioned for Chris to hold it so it did not slam shut.

There were scuffles from the other side.

'Did you hear something…?' he asked. I put a finger to my lips and he fell silent.

Beyond this grille lay another one, making the area between the two approximately the size of a small tray. I hesitantly placed my hand through, and gasped as a rough hand clutched mine.

I heard myself scream, and violently pulled back in an attempt to free myself. 'Let me go! Let me go!' I shrieked. Chris held onto me, trying to pull me back, even though there was absolutely no chance I could be dragged through such a small opening. We screamed in unison until a voice silenced us.

'Jim, Jim, it's you isn't it?' a gravelly voice said urgently.

'It's my dad, it's my dad,' I repeated. He loosened his grip on me and leaned back, eyes wide with shock and fear.

'I knew you'd come back, I knew you wouldn't leave me Jim,' said my dad, almost sobbing. He held onto my hand almost painfully, imploring me not to let go.

'There's a door in the ceiling, that's how you get out. This is where they pass you the food,' I explained. The stuffy, dank air hit me in the face, turning my stomach, and smells I didn't want to identify lingered in my nose.

'The door at the front Jim. That's got to be the way in,' Chris said. 'But the lock…'

'Then find something to break it open!' I yelled at him. 'We can't leave him like this…' Chris got to his feet and began to look around.

'Do you know why you're here?' I turned back to the grille and looked at him. His eyes looked tired and bloodshot. Overgrown and messy hair lay wildly on his head, and his beard was matted with dirt.

'A girl was murdered, like you told me before. I swear Jim, I didn't do it. But I know who did. I swear to God it wasn't me,' he begged.

'But you're connected in some way. Like I was. I was in here and then I got out. I think I broke into the house she used to live in…' I told him.

Chris reappeared and came towards me. 'I can't find anything Jim. But we can come back with the police. We've got enough evidence to go to them now. We can run to the nearest phone box.'

'No, no, no, no…' my dad begged as I withdrew my hand.

'It's going to be okay,' I reassured him. 'We'll be back as soon as possible, and you'll be out by tonight, I promise.' I stood up, letting the grille close behind me. I faintly heard him calling out for me, sobbing pitifully.

The tunnels seemed brighter as I dusted myself off and tried to think where we had passed a phone box. We made our way back to the white door – but it lay wide open, blocked by a man, standing with his arms folded. We stopped dead, and my hand grasped Chris's arm.

Silence hung heavily between us, and we waited for each other to make the first move.

The Chief focused a hard stare on me, then on Chris. He spoke slowly, his voice low and menacing. 'Do you think I don't know you've been following me? Do you think you can intrude in my life and trespass on my private property? Do you know who I am?' Chris and I looked at each other, begging for an answer, a way out.

'You are James Hall. Do you know who I am?' His eyes seemed to burn through me.

'You are the Chief.' My voice was a whisper. He is real. This place is very real.

'And *you*.' He pointed at Chris. '*You* are the one that entered *my* property first. *You* were the one who put *your* hand on the handle of *my* door first.'

Chris had begun to cry, silent tears overflowing from his eyes. He held his hands in front of him, as if he was praying. 'Please, sir, please…' he repeated over and over again.

Ignoring Chris, the Chief turned back to me. 'Jim, Jim.' He shook his head. 'Why did you come back? It's such a shame you're still a few months off your eighteenth birthday. I told my partner we'd not keep a minor. But your friend…' He smiled widely, revealing perfect teeth. He walked towards us and placed a heavy hand on Chris's shoulder, anchoring him to the spot. 'But your friend here, why, you are already eighteen. So I'll have you instead.' He turned back to me. 'You should run Jim, as fast as you can, away from here.' He shuffled back, leaving my exit clear. 'But don't bother about the police. We'll be gone by the time you get back. And your father? You'll find him with a bullet in the back of his head. So I'd run Jim, if I were you I'd run…'

CHAPTER 21

There was another time when I had helped my father with one of his crimes. This time the outcome was far from what he'd planned. I had run away from the scene, soon half staggering as I struggled to get sufficient air into my lungs. Every part of my body ached, and I spotted a low garden wall to sit on – or collapse on. I lowered my head and rested my hands on my knees, like a marathon runner finishing a race, though there was nothing heroic or worthy about me.

The previous evening I had been lying on the living room carpet, rolling a ball to Sally, the only member of the family who lifted my mood. My mother looked on scornfully from the sofa, as though my good mood and the noise I was making were irritating her latest hangover. She sat curled up, cup of something in one hand and cigarette in the other. She always used the same chipped mug, regardless of the drink. I wondered whether this was a crude attempt to disguise the alcohol. When she left the room on one occasion, I sniffed the cup and recoiled in revulsion and surprise; it had been ten o'clock in the morning.

She rose to leave the room before I saw my father. He strode into the room, and it was almost a signal for her to go. I am sure she justified this to herself by thinking if she were not a witness to his conversations, she was an innocent party in his lifestyle.

'Jim.' He motioned for me to stay seated. I immediately felt suspicious; I had been playing with Sally before when he approached me for help with his latest scheme.

'I need you to help me,' he began. He spun a story about some man who owed him money. He and uncle Robin were planning on paying him a visit. He made it sound as though he was doing the right thing and this was the only course of action left. The man had wronged him and he was just taking what was rightfully his. I found myself asking, *who are you trying to convince, me or you?*

'So, me and Robin,' he explained, 'will go to his house tomorrow for a word. You'll be the lookout again, since you did such a good job before.' He smiled, but it didn't reach his eyes. It was a pretence, designed to persuade me to play a part in his seedy activities. But being a lookout was easy, so I found myself nodding in agreement, though I switched off as the storyline unrolled. I even tried to think of the plot twist, but there would never be one in my father's schemes as they were too well planned. If only he put as much energy into creating a family.

So the following evening, I sat on my bike as I had done before. He had fitted a bell, much to my disapproval, since it looked glaringly out of place. But he needed a signal, and the bell was ideal. At first I watched the house, but after a short while my mind began to drift.

Then, out of the corner of my eye, I saw her. Sally. At first she was a small speck in the distance, then I recognised her as she trotted towards me. I got off the bike and crouched down to welcome her, grinning as I ruffled her scruffy coat, her fur coarse against my hands, her tail wagging furiously. She panted and jumped up, covering my face with sloppy dog kisses.

Then I froze. Two men were walking briskly towards the house. They did not see me, and I held onto Sally tightly to avoid drawing attention to us. I watched open-mouthed as the scene unfolded in front of me. The whine of the police sirens grew louder as they approached, and I ducked lower, daring to peek through when I had the chance. Loud voices scared Sally, and she wriggled from my grasp. I frantically gestured to her but didn't dare make a sound. I could only watch as she ran off.

I watched as the police barged into the property and emerged with uncle Robin in a tight hold. He protested loudly, until he was ushered into the nearby police car. I was afraid to move; I held my breath, waiting to see if anyone else came out. The muscles in my legs throbbed loudly until I could take no more. I seized my chance to move and ran, abandoning my bike at the side of the road. My feet pounded the pavement; every step was a step towards safety. I realised I was in serious trouble with my father; it was just his luck to have found a way out before the police got to him.

Back at home, I sat biting my nails, watching the door, awaiting his wrath. But he didn't come home that night, or the next. It wasn't until a week later that I saw him again. I heard him mumbling, but it was too late to retreat. He stood over my mother with an unlit cigarette dangling from his mouth. We looked at each other as the flame of his match burned closer to his fingers. He lit the cigarette and shook the match out.

'Uncle Robin's in prison,' he said flatly. But his eyes said, and it's your fault…

I didn't know what he was expecting from me. I simply nodded and moved towards the cupboard to take out a tin of dog food.

He took a drag on his cigarette, his eyes still on

me. 'I wouldn't bother if I were you.' He blew out a cloud of smoke.

'What...?' I began. Then it dawned, and I pushed the thought away.

'She's not here. Stupid dog was too expensive anyway.' He pushed himself away from the kitchen unit and strode past me. It would be a long time before he asked me to help him again.

CHAPTER 22

I woke up in familiar surroundings, but after the last few weeks' events, it took me a few seconds to work out where I was. I was back home. I stared at the yellowing paint and drab wallpaper. I had left my curtains slightly open and a chink of light shone through. It took an effort to push the duvet off, and when I wandered over to open the curtains fully a bright summer's day greeted me. I pushed open the window and perched on the sill to begin my routine of lighting a cigarette while I thought through my plans for the day. I could see the dustbin lorry in the distance, and heard the faint whine of the mechanisms; it was just another morning.

I exhaled deeply and looked at the cigarette. For some reason, I stubbed it out; I really needed to give up. The wallpaper around the window had begun to yellow. I glanced out of the window again: dog walker, late mother hurrying children into the car for school, neighbour returning from a night shift taking several attempts to reverse park; nothing out of the ordinary.

Downstairs, I was surprised to find my mother

already up. She sat at the kitchen table, still in her dressing gown, her first coffee of the day in front of her.

'You were back late last night,' she said.

I reached for cereal and sat down beside her.

'Hmm,' I nodded. 'I was just out…'

The telephone interrupted me.

'Yeah?' I heard her ask. 'He is… who's this? I'll just get him…it's for you Jim.' She handed it to me.

It was unusual for me to get a call on the landline, and I had a sinking feeling that I didn't want to take the call. I was right.

'Hello?' I croaked, and cleared my throat.

'Jim? It's Chris's mum.' She sounded concerned. 'Were you with Chris last night? He didn't come home. Usually he lets us know but…'

I rubbed my forehead. 'Um… I did see him yesterday. I left him last night…' I paused. I couldn't tell her any more but at least everything I'd said was the truth.

'What time was that?' she pressed me. 'I'm getting quite worried if I'm honest Jim. It's not like him not to call…'

I fumbled for a response. 'He did mention something about a girl? I can't remember her name…'

'Listen Jim, if he contacts you, can you give me a call? In the meantime, I'm going to call a few of his friends…' Her tone told me she meant his *real* friends, not ones like me.

'Of course,' I agreed. I didn't want to hear any more.

'Okay, thank you,' she replied, uneasily.

I put down the phone. His father was a paramedic; if he'd been in an accident dad would've known. That gave me some time…

'Was that Chris Barton's mum?' my mother interrupted.

'Yeah, I bumped into him a while ago…' She didn't appear to want any more details. She tended to stay out of my private life and I intended to keep it that way.

I remembered the last look he gave me: desperate eyes, willing me to save him… I quickly ran upstairs, afraid I was about to throw up. I recalled *his* last words to me: *don't bother going to the police*… But people always said that... He told me not to, but it's what I was going to do. What sane person would leave things the way they were? I dressed hurriedly and left the house.

I felt eyes on me as I walked through the town centre. I was aware that I was probably being paranoid, and no one was really giving me a second glance. This was my only option; there was no way I was going back *there* by myself. The right thing to do was report what had happened in the proper manner.

The police station was empty as I walked in nervously. Behind the counter sat an officer on the phone. He held his hand up, signalling for me to wait. Impatiently, I tapped my foot on the floor. I studied the lanyard around his neck and could see a picture which was obviously taken a while ago as this man had aged considerably since it was new. The name beneath it informed me I was waiting for PC Simon Fowler.

After a few minutes he ended the call, looked up to me and said, 'Yes?'

'I need to see someone,' I blurted. 'I need to report a crime…'

* * *

'So…' he looked up from his notepad. 'To recap, you say there's a factory building with prison cells in it. Your dad and friend are being held there against their will. There are two men running it...?'

I nodded. A huge sense of relief flooded through me. Finally I had been able to tell the whole story to someone in authority. Maybe I should have done this at first, instead of trying to play the hero. But no one will ever believe you, I had told myself. I looked up at the officer and wondered whether he believed me now.

'Hang on one second...' he glanced again at his notes. 'James Hall. I want to run this past my boss...'

I've done my bit, I've done my bit, I convinced myself. There's nothing more I can do for you, Chris... Dad...

There were voices outside the door, which he had left slightly ajar. He was discussing our conversation with a suited man who stood with his back to me. Their voices were hushed, but with every word my vision became clearer. He said don't go to the police and he was right. Had it been some kind of chilling warning...?

'I'll take this from here...' His tone was warm, but it unnerved me.

Dear God, I've walked straight into the lion's den, It's him. With nowhere to run and nowhere to hide, I could only watch as the Chief turned around, walked in and shut the door behind him.

CHAPTER 23

'Did I mention I was in the police force?' he asked, disabling the machine that recorded interviews. 'I wasn't sure if you'd put two and two together. You know, the Chief, and Chief Inspector…?' All I could do was shake my head at him. I regarded him warily, like prey waiting with bated breath for its predator's next move.

'That's why he called me The Chief,' he went on. 'But at one point, I did think it could be one of those…' He waved his hand in front of him, trying to think of the right word. 'What's it called, when the letters in a word all stand for something?' He fixed his stare on me.

'An acronym.'

He barely gave me a chance to answer. 'You know Jim, one of those acronyms. We're in Crenley Hampton, so that's the 'C' and the 'H' of it. I suppose the 'F' could stand for facility, but I can't think of something for the 'I' and the 'E'…' He paused.

He's actually enjoying this, I thought. He's toying with me, and loving watching me squirm…

'How about 'illegal' for the 'I'?' I suggested sarcastically.

He looked at me, a small smile playing on his lips. He was comfortably reclined in his seat. I guessed he must be at least six feet tall, his long legs were crossed under the table and one arm lay on the table. He drummed his fingers on the desk rhythmically and shook his head at me.

'I asked ages ago if you worked for the police,' I heard myself say. 'Ages ago, when your friend let me out. It was one of the first things I asked...'

'Joe you mean? He doesn't work for the police. That's just me. But you've guessed that what we have is nothing to do with the police force...'

'Illegal then,' I muttered to myself. 'And you have my dad in there... and my friend, Chris now...'

'They're both very much alive...'

'But you can't say 'well'? You can't say they are both *well* or *fine* as they obviously aren't. Who would be, after spending a short time with you?'

His lips pursed as he stared at me, saying nothing. After a short time, he spoke, 'You still think he should be out, don't you?'

'My dad? Yes, both of them should be. Him and Chris,' I replied.

'Jim, Jim, Jim...' he muttered, half to himself. 'Okay, I didn't really want to be the one to tell you this but...' He stood up, towering over me. 'Wait here, while I get a file.' He smoothed his tie flat and held his jacket together with one hand before disappearing out of the door.

I frowned, confused. The absurd thought that I should make a run for it popped into my head. He'll rugby tackle you to the floor before you get to the front door, I told myself. I'm in a police station, people saw me come in, so really I'm relatively safe.

His swift return distracted me from any plans to flee. He carried a beige folder to the desk and plopped it down before settling back in his seat. There was a white sticker on the front of the folder, which I didn't have a chance to read before he opened it. There were several sheets of paper inside, an interesting read, I guessed.

'John Hall is your father, yes?' He pulled out a black and white photograph and slid it towards me, rotating it so I could see the image. It was a close-up shot of my father, looking to the right of the camera. He wore a checked shirt, and his trademark cigarette hung from his mouth.

'That's him,' I confirmed quietly.

'And this is also him, yes?' He selected another one and placed it on top of the first. He stood beside a woman, both of them smiling.

'And this?' I barely had time to acknowledge the second one before he laid down a third. This one had been taken at a park; my father pushed a small boy on the swings, and the woman in the second picture stood behind a pushchair.

'The little boy's name is Aaron, I think,' he stated. 'I think it's Aaron...' He glanced at some notes in the folder. 'Yes, he's three. You can't see the baby in this picture, but he's called Eddie...'

I breathed deeply, desperately trying to absorb all this information, and pushed the photos so they lay side by side.

'He's not married to this woman, obviously, as he's still married... to your mum, right?'

I blinked rapidly, suppressing tears. He knew exactly what he was doing and must have known how I would react.

'He doesn't live with her full time, or didn't, I should say, before he came to us.' He rifled through the folder for another sheet. 'Here's his arrest sheet.' He put it in front of me. 'Every crime he's committed is listed there.' He ran his finger down the page, as if to highlight every entry. 'It ends with providing a false alibi. I added that one,' he explained. 'That's one I know he's guilty of, but of course he wasn't punished for it. It's so long-winded going through the proper channels. So much paperwork, so much time wasting...'

I turned my head, fighting back the tears.

'She was a witness for him. She claimed they were at home all night, with the man who stood trial for murdering my daughter. I'm surprised he didn't call on you,' he mused. 'Maybe he'd had enough of you by then.'

I wiped my tears with my sleeve and bowed my head to get away from his mocking face.

'So Jim.' He raised his voice. 'Are you still going to show fierce loyalty to this man? Or do you want me to keep him and throw away the key?'

I sat back in the chair, still averting his gaze. I couldn't think of anything to say. Yes, this man was a terrible father... to me. Yes, he and my mum hadn't provided any kind of stability for me. Yes, he was a seasoned criminal. But I couldn't seem to shake the feeling of what he was going through, where he was at the moment, it just wasn't right. At the end of the day family is family, and whether or not you like what you've got, you can't change it.

I shook my head at him.

Staring at him, I tried to think of the answer he was looking for, an answer that would get me off the hook. 'Throw away the key,' I heard myself speak the words he wanted to hear, that everything he had just revealed about my dad had suddenly hit home and I felt increasing feelings of hatred for him now. I must have sounded more convincing than I felt, as he didn't answer.

He sat there, his eyes boring into me, and I dared to look up. 'What about my friend Chris?' I asked. 'He hasn't done anything wrong.'

'Trespassing on private property, breaking and entering... are you willing to do a swap?' He smiled at me.

I felt disgusted. 'Are you arresting me then?' I

asked in disbelief.

He shrugged. 'Have you committed another crime?'

I genuinely hadn't. I was deliberately keeping a low profile.

He drummed his fingers on the table and gave me a shrewd look. 'Like I said, I'm willing to do a deal with you Jim. Your friend will be free to go if you swap places with him.' Before I had time to answer, he continued. 'Oh, I don't mean a straight swap. You come and work for me, and I'll let him go. It's as simple as that. As for your father, we both know what type of man he is now. I'm offering you the opportunity to oversee his care and ensure that he's not out on the streets to break the law again… or reproduce…'

I sat, processing the ludicrous offer he had just made. He glanced at his watch and stood up, looming over me.

'I've got work to do. You're free to go.' He walked over to the door and held it ajar.

I walked down the corridor a few paces in front of him, past the officer on the front desk, who was now on another phone call. The Chief held the outside door open for me, and the breeze that hit my face had never been more welcoming.

'Oh, and Jim…?'

I turned to face him. He looked slightly awkward.

'When you visited my house, you took a bag from me. It is of great… sentimental value as it was a gift. I'd appreciate it if you could return it the next time we meet. You've got forty-eight hours.' With that, he let go of the door and I stood, completely alone.

* * *

David stood watching Jim from inside the station. He stood almost hunched over before slowly shuffling off in the direction he had just come. He smiled to himself, satisfied that he had Jim exactly where he wanted and soon his plan would all fall into place. Yes it had been his fault that the bag had gone missing in the first place but he was confident that it would safely be in his possession again soon.

He approached Simon on the front desk, now off the phone. David rested his arms on the ledge between them.

'I don't need to remind you that you will forget you ever saw him,' his voice was almost a whisper. There was no response from his colleague, which caused David to narrow his eyes at him.

'Not at all,' Simon muttered. He watched his boss walk back to his office and chewed on his thumb nail anxiously. He planned to confront him that evening – a few phone calls to the right people with tip offs about missing men in the town would land David squarely in the middle of it all and would be something he would not be able to talk himself out of. Checking that David was still in his office, Simon carefully opened the bottom desk drawer. He had stashed a baseball bat and a length of rope. Using a gun posed too many risks, the potential for a witness to hear a gunshot and the evidence that could be traced back to him should it be found. A quick blow to the head followed by bundling David in the back of the transit van he now used seemed more achievable; he would then ensure the back doors were securely tied with the rope before driving the van out of town.

'I'll need your assistance with something tonight.'

David's voice made him jump and he felt his heartbeat quicken. 'Sure, whatever you say,' he heard himself stutter, more eagerly than intended. Anything to get rid of him – David's eyes seemed to penetrate through him at the moment.

He narrowed his eyes at Simon and paused at his desk for a few moments.

'Something else you need?' Simon asked.

He drummed his fingers against a folder which lay on the desk. 'No, as you were,' he finally answered.

Simon closed his eyes and took a couple of deep breaths. He fumbled for the hand held tape recorder in the top drawer and decided to take this with him tonight to strengthen his evidence against his boss.

*　*　*

Later that evening, Simon found himself driving to an address he didn't recognise. It wasn't a house he was heading for as the slip of paper simply told him to take a right turn off the main road heading out of town. David would meet him there. The clock on the dashboard flashed past midnight. Simon found that he lost the traffic and before long, there was no one following him.

He turned the right turn as instructed and instantly the track became uneven. The road surface caused him to rock from side to side almost as if he were driving in a field and the tracks he was using had been made by a tractor. In the distance, he could see a car and the headlights that shone against a building. Simon squinted as though it would help him identify where he was. He reckoned it was an old factory he was heading for. He sighed deeply, David was certainly getting too involved in his covert operations and almost had an air of invincibility about him.

Simon's hand found the sports bag on the seat beside him. He stopped the van deliberately a few yards from David's car and reached into his pocket for the tape recorder. Pressing the record button, he stepped out.

David wore the same coat and hat Simon had come to recognise. He walked towards him until they were a few metres apart, both of them almost taking on the stance of a stand-off.

'Inside here,' David pointed to the ajar door. 'This

particular individual is a nasty piece of work…'

Simon held up one hand, 'I don't need to know.'

The air inside was musty and the small lights on the wall were better than nothing but still gave the place a mysterious feel about it. David led him down a narrow corridor before stopping. The wall he stood in front of had a small grille at floor level.

'He's in here,' David informed him. 'There's an upstairs which opens a hatch in the ceiling. I'll need your help to get him out.'

This was working out better than he thought. He could offer to have the baseball bat to hand in case the prisoner turned on them.

'I've got some restraints in the van,' he spoke quickly, 'and some rope I think.'

'Good, we may need both.'

Simon scuttled back to the van to retrieve his bag. David was waiting at the door and led him to a flight of stairs. After a while, he paused and pressed a button on the wall. Simon watched as a hole began to appear. The flick of a switch illuminated the small space which the man lay in. Simon could see that he was wearing a grey hoodie and was face down.

'He's just asleep,' David informed him. 'You have the rope?'

He bent to retrieve it from the bag.

'Can you secure it to that pipe?' David pointed to the far wall. 'We'll have to make some kind of pulley to hoist him up.'

Simon felt his hands shake as he attempted to tie the stiff rope to the pipe. He tested it and felt the knot tighten.

'You came prepared,' David's voice was monotone. In a swift movement, he kicked the bag towards him. 'And a baseball bat? Very good thinking, you never know when you might need something like this.' He grasped it in his hands as though he were about to take a swing.

Simon remained crouched on the floor and felt the bat against his shoulder. A bizarre thought entered his head that it would almost appear as if he were about to be knighted but knew nothing could be further from the truth.

'Who have you spoken to?' David's voice was urgent as he pressed down on the bat, preventing Simon from standing.

Simon twisted himself awkwardly against the bat so that he turned to face him. 'No one,' he assured him. 'But that doesn't mean that I'm not going to.'

David smiled widely. 'You're going to rat on me, is that it? God, I knew you were up to something. Far too jumpy recently. Christ, you've got to work on how you behave around the office...' he chuckled quietly to himself.

'It's over,' Simon stated firmly. 'I'm done, this is the end, I've had enough.' His voice cracked at the end.

'I can't take it anymore, the lying, the sneaking around. I'm done.' He breathed deeply, waiting for the blow of the bat but nothing came. Simon felt himself shudder as the silence between them became unbearable.

'I can't carry on like this...' his voice trailed off as he heard a faint click from his pocket. He gasped and pressed his hand against it, as though the sound could be muffled but it was too late. The recorder was informing him that the cassette had run out and the machine had turned itself off.

David smiled at him again. 'Oh this is beautiful!' he exclaimed. He held his hand out towards Simon. 'Give that to me...' He jabbed the bat against the side of Simon's head. 'I said...'

Simon muttered to himself and held the recorder up towards him. The tape squeaked as David rewound it and then he heard his own voice playing back his monologue.

'That's quite good, but I think I'll take it from the 'it's over part'. I'll have to do a bit of editing but it will be great as your confession…'

'Christ sake…' he hissed at David. 'You will not get away with murder…'

'I've never murdered anyone and don't intend to…'

'Then just what do you propose to do with me? Shove me in the hole? I've got family who'll come looking for me…'

David shook his head, 'I'm not going to do anything with you…' he bent down and gathered the loose rope off the floor. He pulled on it as Simon had done to test how well it was fastened. Simon watched as he deftly made a loop with the other end of it. He placed the bat under his arm and tied the end of it, making a noose.

'Like I said, I'm not going to do anything to you. You are. This tape will do very well as your suicide note…'

'Jesus, you really are twisted if you think I'm going to…'

'Of course you are, Simon. A clean suicide and a confession to go with it will mean that your family will be in line for your inheritance. Help clear off some of that debt you've got yourself into.' He pulled the noose wide, 'go on.'

Simon's bottom lip trembled as his eyes welled up, 'there's no way,' he shook his head.

David tossed the noose towards him and sighed. 'Of course you will,' he placed the bat in both of his gloved hands again. 'You'll put that on or I will, after I knock you out that is. Then I'll shove you off into the cell. My way will mean you'll feel the pain to your head as I think I'll only hit hard enough to stun you and then push you over. If you do it, you jump and it will be over in an instant. I'll make sure your tape gets left in the right place…' His voice had an impatient tinge to it, as though he was waiting for a child to carry out an unwanted request.

'Do it Simon. You're already in a hole that you can't get yourself out of. I'll just go back to the office and sort out the McGinty case shall I? You'll be arrested before you know it…'

'And you? I suppose you've considered me telling everything I know…'

'No one will ever believe such a ridiculous story. Besides, I know a lot of people in high places, I can easily talk my way out of things…'

Simon sniffed hard and used his sleeve to wipe his eyes.

'Quick suicide and your daughter will get to stay at university. You told me yourself about how she is struggling to pay her fees. This will secure her future…'

He shook his head, 'I can't and won't…'

'Put on the noose!' David shouted at him, causing him to jump. 'I will count and then hit you. I'm rapidly losing my patience. You will jump with a fractured skull at this rate!'

With trembling hands, Simon picked up the other end of the rope. He closed his eyes and slowly put it over his head. He felt David's grip on his arm as he forced him into a standing position.

'You will burn in hell,' he spat scornfully at him.

'Then I'll see you in there,' he guided Simon towards the edge of the hole. He leaned in towards Simon's ear. 'I give you my word that your family will be financially secure.'

Simon closed his eyes and pictured his daughter in his mind. He jumped.

CHAPTER 24

'Why are you here?' The sinister voice with no obvious source boomed into the room. He looked frantically around the bare walls, eyes darting from one to the next. Craig Tremell, aged nineteen, had spent the last few hours asking himself that very question. He couldn't be sure how long he had been in the room, time had dragged so slowly. It was always the same when you were waiting, time seemed to pass slower than normal, as if the hands of a clock struggled to reach the next number or almost wanted to travel backwards.

Since he had woken up in 'the room', he had sat on the mattress, resting against the wall, both arms propped up on his legs. It didn't take a genius to work out why he was here, and though he certainly wasn't a genius he was by no means stupid. His last school report had commented, 'Craig has huge potential, but unfortunately he is easily distracted and has trouble applying himself'. His reports had shown a steady downward trend. He'd had trouble with the work, gradually lost interest, and consequently left school at the earliest opportunity. In the few years since he left, he'd drifted from one job to the next, waiting for the right thing to come along, but it hadn't happened yet. It was this growing frustration and boredom that allowed him to be persuaded to take part in *that* evening. He was convinced that was why he was here now.

He had a wide circle of friends who had attended the same school and lived relatively close to each other. A few of them had gone on to work in construction; one of his friends began working for his uncle, and others were training as mechanics. Craig started work delivering parcels, driving around the same area, working odd days when he was needed.

That night they had been out in a group, celebrating a birthday. He had been designated driver; it was difficult to get a taxi in that part of town. But as the evening progressed, it had become harder and harder to resist alcohol and he'd had a couple of drinks. We'll get a taxi somehow, he told himself. No one will mind if we have to wait a while.

As the lights flashed in the pub to signal closing time, he threw a fleeting look out of the window. Heavy rain had begun to bash against it. They stood under the veranda outside.

'Where's the car Craig?' asked one of his friends.

'We'll have to get a cab, I had a couple of drinks.' But there was a growing queue by the taxi rank in the heavy rain.

'Mate, there's no way we're getting a taxi any time soon,' one of his friends complained. 'How drunk are you anyway? Walk in a straight line for me…' he joked.

Craig found he could do this easily, at least until someone pushed him over. He certainly had not had his usual amount to drink.

'You're fine, where's the car?'

So they piled in, four of them squeezed in the back and one in the passenger seat. Craig took the wheel. He wasn't sure whether the alcohol in his system was making him sleepy as he yawned several times; he shrugged this off and fired up the engine regardless.

'Wait! Pull over!' his friend exclaimed as they passed a drive-through. After a few minutes, the car was laden with burgers and fries. Craig spied a stationary police car straight ahead. He mustered every ounce of composure as he drove past, but to his horror the car's lights sprang to life and it began to follow them at a slow, steady cruise.

'Shhh!' He hissed to his friends so he could concentrate. 'I think this guy's following us.'

'They're after you…' taunted one of his friends.

Their jeers began to get louder, and Craig panicked slightly.

Maybe I shouldn't have got in the car drunk…

Maybe I should pull over…

Maybe I should…

He pressed the accelerator, gently at first, then more urgently. Tightening his grip on the steering wheel, he snaked through the town, turning sharply into side streets. His job meant he knew the streets, knew which road to take, what lay ahead.

'Go on Craig!' the boys urged. The ones in the back seat kept watch for the police car. 'Keep going!' they encouraged him, 'you've nearly lost him.'

He accelerated, and the police car continued its pursuit. His mates banged the seat rest, whooping and cheering as the blue lights and wailing siren began to dim.

'Come on, come on!' they cheered. Craig smirked as he veered round another bend.

Things happened in slow motion. A couple, linking arms, crossed the street ahead. They flashed in front of him, and a woman lurched out of his path. Then he felt the sickening thud.

'Jesus!' He was shaking as adrenaline surged through him, but he did not slow down. 'Did I get him? I mean, did he get up?' he demanded.

'Christ, you need to stop,' one of his back seat drivers urged.

'I think he got up, I'm sure he did,' another said.

Craig continued to drive, and they sat in stony silence for the rest of the journey. The car emptied as he made each drop-off. He bit his lip hard as he pulled out of the last street, alone now. He decided to pull over to inspect the car. Please don't let me see a massive dent, please don't let me see a lot of blood, he prayed.

A quick scan of the car showed a small dent in the bumper, but nothing else. Craig's hand shook as he fumbled for the ignition, then he broke down in uncontrollable sobs. Please let him be okay, he begged. It was a stupid mistake. I'll never drink and drive again. The man will be okay, won't he, probably just a broken leg or something. I've learned my lesson, never again, just give me one more chance, this will ruin me if I'm caught, I'll never work again…

When he arrived home he threw himself down on his bed, weeping silently.

* * *

Craig woke with a heavy head. He squinted in the darkness as pain throbbed in his temples. He staggered to the toilet and crouched in front of it for a while, welcoming the coolness of the floor tiles. He dry heaved a few times into the bowl, while the slow realisation of the previous night slowly seeped into his consciousness. As the truth of what had happened dawned on him, he threw up violently, and slowly drew himself up onto his knees and grasped the sink. He struggled to summon the energy to get off the floor. They'll be banging on the door any moment, he told himself.

Downstairs, he turned on the television, waiting for the local news. Trepidation seared through him. *Knife crime, mayor to open new community centre, cat rescue centre receives grant...* He breathed a sigh of relief as the stories lightened and the tone became cheerier. Nothing... yet.

Craig found himself going through the motions for the next few days. He worked on autopilot, numb, a fake smile on his face. Inside he was tormented; his mind kept flashing back to the thud, to the expression on the man's face, the decision to drive on. This was worse than being arrested; the anticipation of the knock on the door kept his thoughts whirring constantly.

A glance in the local paper a week later turned his stomach. He scanned the story for information, skim-reading to reach the end as soon as possible. *Hit and run victim recovering well... police appealing for witnesses to come forward...* Craig put his head into his hands and began shaking. He's alive, he told himself. I got away with it. That's the last time I ever drink, I promise. From now on, it's a new start...

* * *

Craig looked up at the tannoy, which was obviously the origin of the voice.

'Why are you here?' it demanded.

Craig sank to his knees, hands clasped in front of him. 'I hit a man with my car. I'd been drinking. I'm so truly sorry... if I could turn back the clock...' his voice trailed off, tears coursing down his cheeks. 'I'm so sorry,' he whispered, not sure if anyone could hear him. He placed his palms on the concrete floor and dropped on all fours. From behind him he heard a loud click, and turned around to see a metal grille on the floor sliding back. Puzzled, he walked over to it and pulled out a tray with a sandwich and a cup of water on it. He warily raised the cup to his lips and welcomed the cool water. The sandwich had a cheap artificial tasting cheese centre but he ate it gratefully.

'Thank you,' he muttered, to no one in particular.

Suddenly, the hiss of the tannoy again.

'Craig Tremell, you are in a holding facility for the crime of a hit and run on Saturday 5th April of this year. You are very lucky that we got to you first. Listen very carefully. There *are* no second chances. Commit a second crime and we'll find you and bring you back here. You'll stay here until the day you die. Do you understand?' The voice crescendoed.

Craig nodded furiously.

That was the last thing he remembered before lying down on the dirty mattress, his head throbbing and vision blurring like the start of a bad migraine. The sound of farm animals roused him; his mouth felt dry as he woke, confused, to find he was in the middle of a field. He shuffled into a sitting position, frantically looking around for any clues to where he was. He gingerly stood up and began to walk towards the road at the edge of the field. He stumbled slightly; his shoes felt loose, and he saw his shoelaces had been removed.

CHAPTER 25

I was uncomfortable dressed in the crisp white shirt and tie, and kept pulling at the collar. The buttoned-up shirt and the constricting tie felt alien; it was a long time since I had dressed so smartly. But it was a condition of the job that I dressed this way, with neatly pressed trousers as well. What's the point anyway? I asked myself. It's not as though anyone is going to see me.

'Stop pulling on it,' he scolded me. 'It's as though you've never had to dress properly before.'

The dress code had been part of my 'induction' when I arrived. The uniform had been the least of my concerns over the last few days. I had wrestled with many feelings since leaving the police station. *You have forty-eight hours*, he had informed me. It was no exaggeration to say that I had spent nearly all of that time deciding what to do. I had gone to report the factory and the kidnapping of my dad and friend to the police, only to find out that the Chief *was* the police. How could I possibly take matters any further when it turned out that the very people who were supposed to protect me were corrupt? I could've just walked away, made a new life for myself in another town. They said themselves that they were 'cleaning up one town at a time,' so I could've moved far up north and saved myself all this. But at the end of the day I couldn't live with the guilt. Chris had been taken because of me. It was *my* fault that he was where he was. So I had no option: I would say yes to the Chief. But when the time was right… I wasn't entirely sure what I would do, but I was quite determined that this would not be the end. I would get my revenge. Some day.

I had gone back to the police station exactly two days later, carrying the bag that he had insisted I bring. At first I had been unable to find it, but I located it stuffed far under my bed. My mother no longer went into my room, but I didn't want to risk her seeing it as it looked out of place among my things. I hadn't broken the lock as I'd intended to. The Chief could have it back if it was so precious to him, and I figured that might score me some points in the long run.

He'd been behind the front desk, leaning over the computer when I walked in.

He raised his eyebrows as I approached. 'James Hall. I'm not surprised to see you. Thank you for being so… punctual,' he remarked. 'I'll be with you in a few minutes. Please take a seat.'

I wandered over to the seating area but felt too restless to sit, so I studied the posters on the wall, urging the public to be more vigilant, to report any suspicious activity. I scoffed. If only people knew the truth.

He snapped me out of my thoughts. 'James, would you like to come through?'

I followed him to the same room as before. We sat at opposite sides of the desk again.

'Thank you for returning my bag,' he smiled, running his hands over it. 'So, you've come to a decision?' he asked.

'Yes, that's why I'm here…'

'Probably the right choice,' he smirked. 'I really think you'd find it hard to stay out of trouble. You'll be in the best place. Remember what I said would happen if you ever...'

I held up my hand, signalling for him to stop. 'So what happens now?'

He stared at me and folded his arms. 'Okay, I'm going to give you an address. I want you to be there at nine thirty tonight. Once we arrive at the facility, I'll fill you in completely about procedures, duties, etc.' He reached into a drawer for some paper, took a pen from his jacket pocket and he wrote an address in neat script before sliding it over to me. 'Here, at nine thirty,' he repeated. 'Pack a few personal items but don't go mad. We have plenty of supplies. No phone or other electrical items.'

I looked at the address but did not recognise it.

'It's on the far side of town,' he said. 'You'd best get a taxi.' He pushed the chair back and stood up. I looked up at him, surprised.

'Is that it?' I asked.

'For now.' He held out his hand. 'It's been a pleasure James.' His handshake was firm and business-like. 'I look forward to working with you.'

***

I cast a long look around my bedroom as I folded some clothes to pack into the bag on my bed. I wasn't sure exactly what to take but told myself if I'd forgotten anything important, I'd come back and get it.

'Where are you off to?' a voice barked.

I jumped. My mother stood in the doorway. I felt as though I'd been caught doing something illegal.

'Uh,' I struggled. 'I'm just going to see a few friends.'

She seemed satisfied with this, and turned to leave. I watched as she reached the top of the stairs. 'Oh Jim...'

she shouted. 'While you were out, Chris's mum called, *again*. She's going to the police. Apparently, he's not been seen for days. For Christ's sake, stop her calling here…'

Chris's name sent a chill down my spine. I sat on the edge of my bed for a moment, head in my hands, listening to her heavy footsteps down the stairs. If only you knew, I thought.

The rest of the afternoon seemed to drag. I pondered the contents of my bag. Should I pack some kind of weapon? I dismissed the thought; what if they caught me with it?

Just before nine o'clock I called for a taxi and sat silently in the back, staring out of the window as the world rushed by, a blur of colours.

'Meeting someone?' asked the driver.

'Hmm?' I didn't really want to engage in conversation.

'You'll be miles from anywhere. Have you got anyone to meet you?'

'Yes I have,' I confirmed.

Outside grew more industrial; grey buildings lined the road and an occasional car drove past. I had no idea where I was going from here, as I paid the driver and stood at the corner of the street. Why was I here? What was so important about these buildings? I checked my watch: 9:28. There was absolutely no one around. I repeatedly checked until the time read 9:32. I wasn't late; maybe he'd changed his mind?

I turned sharply as I heard the steady crunch of footsteps. A figure strode towards me, hands in pockets and a cap with the peak pulled down shielding his eyes. I held my breath as he grew closer, and expected him to speak, but he walked straight past me. Confused, I watched him go, and heard nothing behind me, not even when a sharp blow made me crumple to the pavement.

I woke on a hard bed. The mattress felt too firm and the thin blanket too scratchy. There was a dull ache in my head.

'Sorry about that,' said a voice. 'You could call it payback.'

I turned to see Mr Greasy Hair sitting beside me. In his hand was a flannel, which he laid on my aching head. It felt cool and welcome.

'Again, I'm sorry. It was necessary. You can't know where we are.'

'The old factory building…' I began.

He shook his head. 'This place is our permanent prison. The old one became… unusable,' he explained. 'This is the holding facility where you were a prisoner.'

I looked away, still confused. Were my dad and Chris even in this building, or was I being fed a pack of lies? I cast my mind back to what I had seen after I knocked Mr Greasy Hair unconscious. The place I had seen my dad when I had been with Chris bore no resemblance. So what was going on? I pressed the flannel on the lump on my head. It didn't feel as bad as I expected.

'What do I call you?' was all I could think of to say.

'Joe,' he said, simply. 'No secret, it's my real name.'

I pushed myself up to look at the rest of the room. It was small and vaguely familiar.

'Been here before, haven't you?' he smiled. 'This was my room. You visited it.'

I breathed deeply as I recognised the same desk, the same pictures. Emily smiled at me, and 'Bakerfield's Best Catch' stood out boldly. 'This is your room?' I asked.

'It's yours now,' he answered. 'I'll remove those pictures.'

At the side of the desk stood the bag I had packed at home, now unzipped. I chose not to comment on this.

'There's a bathroom through there.' He gestured to the door next to the bed. 'You'll find a shower in there, everything you need. I'll leave you to get yourself sorted.' He stood up to leave. 'Oh, and the wardrobe.' It was a small, single old-fashioned wooden one. He walked over to it.

'There's your uniform.' He opened the door to reveal a row of white, short-sleeved shirts, some pairs of trousers and a tie rack with an assortment of neutral coloured ties.

I reached over the bed and pulled my bag towards me. It was practically empty. 'I packed more than this,' I muttered. All I could see were toiletries.

He shrugged. 'That's because you don't *need* anything else.'

'But what about when I go out?' I asked, confused. 'I can't wear the uniform all the time, surely?'

He smiled at me, but it seemed artificial. 'James, there is no going out. You work here now, you eat here and you sleep here.' He turned towards the door. 'Like I say,' he added, 'get yourself freshened up and I'll be in the office when you're ready.'

I sat still, fear washing over me. What had I got myself into?

CHAPTER 26

The door creaked as I pushed it open. I walked along the corridors, still as uneasy as the first time I was here. It's the unknown, I told myself. I may be wearing the uniform and be on the other side now, but I still have no idea what is going to happen next. Everything was new, the shirt and trousers, the shiny black shoes. I'd had trouble fastening the tie; it wasn't as though I had worn one on a regular basis. The door to the office was ajar, and I could see Joe sitting on one side of the desk, just like before.

He stood up as I approached, and beckoned me. 'Everything okay?' he asked, walking round the desk.

I nodded unenthusiastically, and shuddered as he raised both hands, anticipating his vice-like grip around my neck.

'Relax,' he laughed, and adjusted my tie. 'I bet you've never worn one of these before,' he mumbled. 'Except perhaps in court?'

I pursed my lips and breathed deeply, not taking the bait.

'There.' He smoothed down my shirt collar with a satisfied look. 'You'll do. Please sit James.' He pointed at the chair. I sat, finding it as intimidating as before. On the desk lay several beige folders and a large, folded sheet of paper.

'Do you prefer James or Jim? And don't look so nervous. You work here now.'

'James.' I wasn't even sure if this was true.

He unfolded the sheet of paper and slid it over to me. 'This is a map of this building,' he explained.

This was interesting. There were two sketches, drawn very neatly, as if prepared by an architect. 'Like a blueprint?' I asked.

He nodded and pointed to one of the pictures. 'This is the floor we're on at the moment. It's the ground floor.'

I thought back to the factory Chris and I had visited, where I'd seen my dad through the grille. It wasn't something I wanted to dwell on so I focused back on the sketch. It was circular as I had expected; I'd had a feeling I was running in a circle as I'd desperately looked for a way out. I traced my finger over the other drawing, trying to figure out what it was.

He seemed to read my thoughts. 'This level is underground,' he explained. 'All the cells are underground, with an access hatch in the ceiling. All are inhabited now, except for these two.' He pointed to two adjacent cells. I looked up, waiting for him to continue.

'This cell has a proper flight of stairs down to it.' He pointed to the last square on the diagram. 'It's the only way down to the cells. It's where food is carried down...'

His voice trailed off, and I swallowed hard, still uncomfortable about the whole set-up. 'And this cell?' I asked. 'You said it was empty?' I tapped it.

'That was Chris's cell. We're true to our word James. You're here now and he's not. We let him go. I mean, we transported him to a safe place. I'm sure by now he's found his way home and… is ready to start the rest of his life. This place will be just a horrible memory for him.'

My thoughts returned to the factory. This map certainly didn't correspond with what I had seen. My father had been on ground level not underground.

I decided not to dwell on this. 'Safe place?' I heard myself say.

'Just outside his home town. We're not mean. When you went back, you had no money, right?'

I frowned.

'No way of getting home if we'd left you miles away. I bet it was just a short walk back, once you'd got your bearings.'

The open field I had woken up in, the steady hum of the tractor, the farm buildings in the distance… The Chief travelling to a factory every day, my father's cell in that building? I had a niggling doubt: something wasn't sitting right…

'Are we the only people you've ever let out?' I asked.

He breathed deeply. 'No,' he replied, after a long pause. 'Others… have been released. You've no need to worry about that though.'

'Who?'

He seemed to have drifted off, deep in thought. He shook his head and blinked, as if to rid himself of a cloud of smoke.

'A young chap, made a very silly mistake. We had him for a very short time, as that was all he needed. This rehabilitation does work, you see, James.' He sounded a little smug, as if he and the Chief had found the cure for all of society's problems while the rest of us walked around naïvely, refusing to acknowledge their oh-so-simple solution.

'He's now living a normal life back in his home town. I think he's at college, eventually hoping to be a vet or something…' He scratched his chin and his voice trailed off.

'You keep tabs on him?' I asked.

'I do checks from time to time, to see that he's okay, and living a crime-free life.'

I had to glance away, he looked so self-satisfied. 'Anyway, back to the matter in hand?' He clearly did not want to talk about this any more. 'Your duties will start with the food preparation, I'll show you where, and you'll deliver the food through the hatches. I'll oversee the... wells. I don't think you're ready for that yet. You'll also monitor the prisoners' behaviour via the screens in the back room.' He gestured behind him without looking round. 'You'll note anything of interest in the log books, I'll show you where and how. That's about it, for now. I'll stay on site for a couple of days until you get into the swing of things, and then I'll leave you to it.'

It seemed well thought out and very final.

'Where will you go?'

'Home, I guess. Don't look so worried, you'll be fine. I've done this job for a long time myself.'

'But never getting out? You said I'd be in here all the time.' My voice rose, agitated.

'In time, perhaps. When you've earned our trust. But it's me who'll have the final say. As for the Chief, well, I doubt you'll see him again.' This chilled me. I wanted to know why, but couldn't bring myself to ask.

We went through to the surveillance room. Joe reached down to the access panel under the desk and activated the screens. I quickly counted the thirteen active cells he had talked about – *all are inhabited now* – and my eyes scanned rapidly for my father's.

'We have other...guests now,' he explained.

'And they are all in the cells at the moment?'

'Yes. We have a few in the wells, as we call them. They are reserved for our more serious offenders. You have the cameras for them too.'

I didn't want to know about the wells; I recalled his

chilling threat the last time I was here. I cast my eyes over the paraphernalia on the desk and focused on the tannoy system in the centre of it. It looked like an old-fashioned device with a large, red button; I presumed this was pressed to speak and released to hear an answer. He saw me looking at it.

'Oh, and James?'

I looked up.

'Whatever you do, don't, and I repeat don't, ever push the red button.'

I looked at it and then back to him quickly. 'You're going?' I asked desperately. 'What if I get bored?'

He smiled at me and disappeared back into the room we had just come from. I didn't follow him but could hear him rummaging around for something.

'Here,' he tossed a newspaper in my direction. 'I can bring you them from time to time, so you can keep up to date with what's going on. I'll bring you some books too.'

He left not long after. I sat in the office staring at the front of the newspaper but for some reason, none of the words were registering. Then I saw it. A small box in the corner of the page, indicating that this was a story which the paper hadn't much information on yet but was serious enough to have made the front page. I felt my blood run cold as I scanned the story: Unidentified body of policeman discovered in apparent suicide.

CHAPTER 27

The building stood inconspicuously on the edge of an industrial estate. Surrounding units were occupied, and included a car rental company, farm equipment hire firms, various warehouses, garages and shops selling tools to the public. Lorries passed through every day; from early in the morning, their steady hum could be heard in a nearby housing estate. The industrial estate was accessed by a road which was the first exit on a roundabout on the way out of town.

The road leading into the industrial estate had speed bumps at regular intervals, to discourage cars from racing through and ensuring lorries travelled carefully. The road surface was littered with potholes and cracks. Many people in the town were employed there, and others travelled from neighbouring towns on a bus which stopped at the top of the housing estate.

David purposely arrived several minutes early, in order to have a good look round on foot. He had driven around the area many times, but preferred to get a feel for it by taking a stroll around the warehouses. Lighting a cigarette, he stood in front of the building and looked up and down. It was grey and blue and stood two storeys high. A sign outside said it had once been used for self-storage. Outside there was parking for many cars, and he reckoned that transit vans or small lorries would be able to park comfortably too. He had driven through a large grey gate; he guessed it could be fitted with number plate recognition equipment.

From the corner of his eye he saw a car approaching, and turned to watch as it drove past the small road. There was a small burger van just to the left, and two cars were currently parked there. He heard another car approach before he saw it: a black estate car, which signalled to turn into the small road and pulled up outside the building, next to his car. A young man got out and smoothed down his trousers before walking towards him.

'David Foster?' he asked, holding out his hand. David shook it briefly, and the man began to unzip a folder he was carrying. 'I hope you haven't been waiting too long?'

David shook his head. 'I was early. I wanted to have a look around the area.'

'It's fairly busy on the main road, but this unit won't get much through traffic.' He waved a hand towards a warehouse opposite. 'They relocated last month.' He looked back at the building they had come to see. 'Would you like to have a look inside?'

'I'm waiting for a colleague,' David replied, checking his watch. He looked around again. 'The fencing?' he asked.

'Surrounds the entire perimeter,' came the reply. 'There is full CCTV, and the units benefit from high security as each is individually alarmed...'

Another car headed towards them and pulled up. Joe stepped out, looking slightly agitated. 'My apologies,' he offered.

'Not to worry, I've not been here long myself,' David answered.

They followed the man inside the building. David turned to look at his friend, who was dressed more smartly than usual. 'Going somewhere?' he whispered, more out of humour than genuine interest.

'Just out with friends,' he replied, trying to sound casual, and quickly changed the subject. 'The sizes of each unit?'

'They range from fifty to four hundred square feet,' the man confirmed, checking his folder. 'There's a large warehouse area, and each unit is accessed by a PIN code, did I already mention that?' He continued before they had a chance to answer. 'Smoke and fire alarms, full privacy for each unit and it's well lit. Would you intend to keep it as a self-storage facility?'

'Possibly, with a few alterations,' David replied. He turned to look at Joe, his face giving nothing away. They stopped to look at a small unit. From the outside, it looked no bigger than a garage. It was well presented, secure but was obvious that it had been disused for a while. A small pile of yellowing newspapers was stacked haphazardly in one corner, and the air smelled musty.

'Staff area,' the man indicated as they walked past an open space. 'Obviously you'd set your own opening hours if you were intending to keep it as a storage facility for the public, and you'd want to keep someone on site the whole time.'

David nodded. The man continued his sales pitch but he had tuned out. He had already made up his mind about the building.

'Thank you, we'll be in touch shortly,' he smiled, grasping the man's hand and giving it a firm shake.

'So...?' He looked at Joe, and they began a gentle stroll around the car park, staying close to the front of the building.

'Are you asking for my opinion, or just

agreement?'

'Both… Neither.'

'You can't be serious,' Joe reasoned. 'I mean, look where we are. It's worse than what we've got at the moment! Right on the edge of a housing estate, five minutes from town, not to mention slap bang in the middle of a busy industrial estate!'

'But it's perfect,' David replied coolly. 'The units are the right size and we'd need to do a few alterations, but we have the time. Just think – our third prison…'

'And who will run this place? You?'

'Yes. I want you to stay at Crenley. We've done a lot there, and now it's time to start somewhere else. It feels like it's yours anyway, since you've been there the longest.' He paused. 'How is *he* doing?' Joe looked quizzical and David mistook his silence for ignorance. 'I mean James. How is he doing?'

'He's fine,' Joe answered flatly. 'Following instructions, but not exactly what I'd call intuitive…'

'He stole my bag. That's quite intuitive enough.'

'He had no idea what he was taking, and oddly enough he didn't break into it,' Joe replied. 'Don't worry, I can assure you there was no dye under his fingernails the first time he came back. That would have taken several days to wash off. You saw him yourself. Strange, he has no idea what he's got himself into…'

He considered what David was suggesting for this place. He wasn't exactly overjoyed at the prospect of expanding their enterprise. There were too many risks involved.

'Do you trust him?'

'James? Not one bit,' Joe answered. He didn't even have to think about it. 'I don't trust him at all.'

David pursed his lips. 'Then put him back in a cell if you've had enough of him. I don't think he's serving any purpose.'

* * *

Joe sat in a bar later that evening, alone, gazing into his glass and mulling over his conversation with David, already on his second drink. It was fairly crowded for a week night. He had deliberately chosen a bar in a different town, a more sophisticated place than he would normally pick. He adjusted his cufflinks, probably for the hundredth time since he'd sat down. Nerves, he told himself. When was the last time you went into a bar alone? Not since Amanda, and certainly not while he was having secret meetings with Jill. God, I hate this, this feeling, he thought, sighing into his beer. But now that he had James to run the facility, it was time to venture out, to meet someone again and start a new chapter in his life. It was about time.

Joe hadn't dared to work out exactly how long he'd been looking after the facility. Ever since David had found out about the affair, the night of Emily's death, he'd almost felt like a prisoner himself in that place. It must have been years since he'd been out; he had almost felt the sunshine biting into him when he saw daylight again. The town had undergone a few changes since he'd last visited. A few new bars and restaurants had sprung up.

He spotted her sitting alone at the other end of the bar. For a moment he was taken back; he caught a glimpse of her hair, golden and glinting under the decorative lights. *Jill.* It took him a moment to realise that it wasn't her but someone who bore a remarkable resemblance. She was dressed in a smart creamy white linen suit. He looked down at his own outfit, dark jacket and trousers to match, dark shirt with no tie. Here goes nothing, he thought and walked over to her seat.

He picked up a cocktail menu from the bar beside her glass. He allowed himself to look at her and broke into a smile as she met his gaze.

'I've got no idea what half these drinks contain,' he laughed. 'I mean, who can tell what you're getting from the name?'

She cleared her throat politely and replied, 'And you just try asking for some of them with a straight face.'

'*What* on the beach?' Joe dropped the menu in mock shock-horror. He shook his head. 'Can I buy you a proper drink?'

She looked at her empty glass and nodded, smiling. 'Okay thank you.'

He summoned the bartender and ordered two more drinks, then pulled up a stool and sat next to her. 'Do you…' He laughed as he realised what he was about to ask.

'Do I…?'

'I was going to say 'come here often', but that is probably the worst line ever. It's just that I'm new to the town and it's my first visit here.' He paused and took a breath. 'Is it usually this busy for a Wednesday or…?' *Stop, for heaven's sake, you're rambling.*

'We're near the theatre and there's a show on tonight,' she explained. 'Listen, um…' She tossed her hair, *just like Jill*, and smiled a little too sympathetically. 'I'm actually meeting someone…'

'Oh.' The mirrored tiles at the back of the bar were a mocking witness to how badly this was going.

'And now I've made you uncomfortable.' She began to slide off her stool.

'No, please…' He downed his drink much faster than he wanted to. 'I need to be off anyway.' He nodded towards her, avoiding eye contact. 'It was lovely to meet you. Whoever he is, he's a very lucky guy.' He turned away and walked swiftly to the door.

Outside, the evening breeze danced around him. That had been much harder than he remembered. He headed off, anywhere, just away from that bar.

* * *

And so began the new chapter in my life. I ate, I slept, I fed the prisoners, then repeated the cycle. There were bedpans – they had no toilets – which I had to empty too. I did my jobs as quickly as possible, and began to hate the sound of my own footsteps. Silence hung ominously over everything. I didn't like the feeling of being alone underground, even though the prisoners were only on the other side of the carefully cemented walls. It was too quiet: the cells were obviously well soundproofed. I hovered outside one evening, desperate to hear some sign of life but at the same time afraid I would.

It was my reluctance which broke the cycle of delivery of food trays that evening.

Joe had shown me how to extract the old tray and replace it with the new one quickly, so there was no time for the prisoner to react. He had obviously perfected this fluid movement over time. As I knelt outside a cell, a metal hatch on my side and the grille in the cell was all that separated me from the stranger on the other side. I looked down at the tray and went through the process. The old tray was always in the gap; it appeared the prisoners had been warned that its absence meant no more food. I slowly pushed in the tray, but held the hatch open for a few moments. Then I heard him.

'Please,' he rasped. 'I just want to talk.'

I gasped and jerked backwards, my fingers curled under the hatch opening. The voice chilled me, but not as much as when it had been my father on the other side. I took deep breaths to compose myself before slowly resuming my original position. I pulled the hatch as wide as it would go and found that it made an almost perfect ninety-degree angle with the floor.

It was dark on his side of the cell but the sound of his voice told me he was close to the grille. The light was dim on my side so it took me a few moments to make out his hand pressed against the grille and his face behind it.

'Who are you?' he asked.

I willed myself to snap back the hatch and bolt towards the stairs, but for some reason I did neither. I opened my mouth to speak but could only stutter back at him, 'I... I...'

'You're not *him*.'

'Who do you mean?' I replied after a while. Joe had instructed me to never push the button, and almost petulantly I told myself what I was doing now wasn't disobeying. All the same, I was sure I was still breaking the rules.

'You're someone different. He doesn't behave like you. He never says anything.'

'Joe...' I glanced towards the stairs, afraid he might appear at any moment.

'Is he your boss or something?' the prisoner continued. 'He's not going to let me out, is he? How long have I been in here, do you know?'

I breathed hard, trying to estimate how long had passed since I was in here myself. I recalled there had only been the three of us then.

'A couple of months, I think.'

He bowed his head slightly and I averted my eyes. 'Is that all?' His tone was much quieter now. 'What is this place anyway? Is it a secret organisation?'

I shook my head. 'No, it's a prison. I can't get you out. I can't get anyone out. I don't even know how to...' My voice trailed to a stop as he moved his head away from the grille.

Eventually he spoke again. 'I thought it was just a rumour...'

I struggled to form a coherent reply. 'What rumour?'

'Mate of mine, said he'd been in a prison. He's spent time in and out anyway, like me, but he said this one was different. God knows how, but he's managed to stay out of trouble since then. The only thing was, he was told if he's caught again, they'll come for him and he'll be back here for good.'

'What's your name?' I asked.

'Anthony. You?'

'James,' I replied.

'Can't you just get him? I mean, jump on him and get his keys, force him to let you out. You've more of a chance than anyone else…'

'I can't,' I interrupted him. 'Look… it's difficult. There's more to it than that. If I do… I don't know what will happen…' I was conscious I was revealing too much. 'He knows my family,' was all I could offer.

'What's the point of me going back outside anyway?' he said miserably. 'I'd probably end up behind bars again whatever. Whether it's a normal prison or here.'

I shuffled back. 'I can't talk to you any more. I shouldn't have said anything in the first place. If he finds out…'

'No, don't go!' He sounded panicked. 'Look James, if you ever get out of here, my mate I told you about? His name's Isaac Watkins. He's got connections, might be able to help you sort this guy out…'

I nodded, not sure how far the Chief's net was cast. I made a mental note to remember this name regardless.

'So you can't get me out James? Maybe we could have a chat to him together. There must be a way into this room…' He turned around, but with no light it was pointless.

'I told you I can't. I just can't,' I repeated quietly. I lowered the grille slightly.

'No… no… no!' he urged. He hooked his fingers into the grille again, in a vain attempt to get closer to me. 'Can you get me something? Please?'

His eyes blinked rapidly. 'Please can you get me a knife, the sharpest you can find, please James?'

'You'll never get the chance. You'll never get close

enough to him.'

'It's not for him,' he replied flatly. 'I never said it was. I can't stay here like this…'

I shook my head vigorously. 'I can't do that, I just can't…'

'Please James, please!' He was almost shouting now. 'What is it to you anyway? What does it matter to you? If you can't get me out, at least give me a chance…'

That was enough. I pulled my hand away and felt the hatch snap shut. The sharp click cut Anthony's tirade off mid-flow. I stood up and limped towards the steps, trying to shake off the cramp in both legs. By the time I reached the light switch, I was running; I flicked it off and pelted up the stairs.

In the surveillance room there was a large blue ring binder by the video players, used to record any interesting actions from the prisoners. I was alone now; Joe left every night, always ensuring he locked the door behind him. The exit to the prison was via a door on the ground floor, in a large storage room containing filing cabinets. I had seen a glimpse of it one evening as Joe left, but I had no idea how the outside door was secured.

I sat in the comfortable black leather chair facing the television screens, swivelling from side to side. The tannoy was positioned temptingly in front of me. I had been warned never to touch the button, and so far I had obeyed. I desperately tried to justify my actions from a few minutes ago. Not pressing the button wasn't difficult; even though I could see my dad on the screen, I had no idea what I'd say to him. He'd ask me when I was going to get him out – and I did not even know the answer to when I was going to get out. Besides, in the light of what I'd learned about him, I wasn't sure how I felt any more. For the moment at least, I'd decided my best course of action was to conform to all the rules and see where it took me.

Blue ring binder. I leafed through it looking for clues. It did not make for exciting reading. Earlier pages were written in note form, with lots of abbreviations. *Prisoner 1 – arr. 02.45, very agitated state, 10 ml given at 02.45…* I didn't recognise the name of the drug. Was it a sedative used to shut him up? The date of this prisoner's arrival was a few years ago; it obviously wasn't my dad's record.

Prisoner two's first entry was more recent. The date appeared to tally with my calculations of when my dad went missing. One section of information caught my eye: he'd been given a lot of sedatives on many different occasions. I wondered why. The only thing I could think of was that perhaps he'd been particularly difficult when he was in withdrawal from nicotine, alcohol and whatever other drugs he'd taken on the outside.

At the very back of the binder was information on captives who I could not link to the prisoners on the monitors. They were labelled A to K, and each was named. Each data set ended with 'd' apart from the last one, Prisoner K, who was marked 'r'. I ran through every word I could think of beginning with 'd' and 'r', and decided on a few which seemed to be the best fit. Detained? Deported? Discharged? Relocated? Reoffended? Released?

I heard the sound of a key in a lock, and quickly snapped the folder shut. A sense of guilt washed over me even though I was not doing anything wrong. Joe strutted into the room, looking agitated.

'Anything to report?' he asked, shrugging off his jacket.

I quickly looked him up and down. He looked too smartly dressed for this visit. For a moment, I dared to wonder where he'd been, what kind of a life he had on the outside.

'No, nothing,' I answered, as flat as his mood. I turned back to the screens and glanced at my watch. It was approaching ten o'clock, but I was sure the concept of night and day was long gone for the prisoners. Many of them were lying down, but I knew first-hand that there was nothing else to do but be alone with your thoughts as the hours and days dragged by.

'Good. You can have a drink with me then.' He went into the adjoining room and sat down in his chair to rifle through the drawer. 'James?'

I raised my eyebrows as he placed a bottle of expensive whisky on the desk. I didn't need to be asked twice. I sat opposite him as he poured a generous amount into two glasses.

He held up the glass with a 'cheers,' and threw it back in one go. I gingerly took a sip. Spirits had never really been my thing, but I wanted to keep him sweet.

'Bad night?' I spoke carefully, aiming to come across as a concerned friend ready to agree as he put the world to rights. He shook his head and poured another glass.

'Just... no, nothing.' His gaze drifted away and I smelled his aftershave. It was overpowering, but by now I would have been sensitive to any fragrance. In a show of solidarity, I threw my own drink back, hoping he didn't notice my grimace.

'Wow,' was all I could say. The whisky buzzed warmly in my throat.

'Good stuff, eh?' He reached to pour me another. 'You've no idea how many nights this stuff has got me through.' He was slurring his words slightly. 'So James, how are you finding your new job?' He let out a small laugh.

'Well, I... it's different,' was all I could think of. How many has he had? I wondered. Then I had a lightbulb moment. Maybe the question I should ask was could I get him to talk?

'What more could I ask for?' I went on. In a moment of courage, I picked up the bottle and refilled his glass myself. 'I mean, free lodgings, space and time to think, and most important of all...' I ensured I held his gaze before adding, 'all the cheese sandwiches I could ever wish for.'

He chuckled, and held his tumbler close to his chest. 'I'll drink to that James.' He waved his glass high in the air. 'To processed cheese…'

'To cheese.' I clinked glasses with him and joined in with his laughter. 'So.' I cleared my throat a few times. 'I was recording the data, as you requested…'

'In the file,' he added.

I nodded. 'There are a few pages in the back?'

'In the back?' He rubbed his temple. 'Oh, that. They're probably just notes from the other batch…' He drifted off and I willed him on to continue.

'Other batch?' I asked, hoping to sound curious and not desperate.

'We had another group of prisoners once, in our first prison, before this lot. Call it a trial run. It went horribly wrong though.'

'They didn't stage a mutiny, did they? Protest over the limited catering?' I tried to come across as light-hearted. Anything just to keep him talking.

He smiled. 'No, we killed them all. They're all dead.'

I gasped, and froze for a moment. His tone, his facial expression remained neutral; I couldn't decide if this was some cruel joke, or he was being deadly serious. Either way, both he and the Chief were very dangerous. I was glad I was sitting down, because all of a sudden I felt light-headed and sick, from the drink and from what I was hearing. Deceased, departed, dead: however you wanted to dress it up, the 'd' in the files stood for dead.

Except one.

'All of them?' I asked. 'Every last one?'

'All except one. We released him before the others died. He was saved… lucky for him…' He slowed down as he stifled a yawn. He lay back in his chair and I saw his eyes were closing.

'Craig. Was that his name? Craig Tremell?'

'Yep, that was him…' He was already more than half asleep.

I moved to grab the glass before it tumbled from his grasp. His breathing slowed as he fell into a drunken sleep.

As quietly as I could, I pushed my chair back and stood up, carefully placing the glass on the desk. I looked at him with contempt. You don't know how much you've given me, I mentally scolded him. Craig Tremell, the model student at college, the only other prisoner I knew of who had been released, other than Chris and me. And now I had a set of keys and access to the forbidden room, so a hefty dose of sedative for Joe would give me time to find the answers I was looking for.

CHAPTER 28

He lay spread-eagled in the chair, his breathing heavy and eyelids twitching. His head was tilted to one side and lips parted slightly. I allowed myself to study him. He had recently had a haircut which made him look very ordinary; only the scar under one eye distorted his face. I took a step towards him, expecting to see a set of keys fastened to a clip on his belt loop, as I'd seen in films. I was disappointed. Then I remembered he'd been wearing a jacket; I saw it from the corner of my eye, hanging on the back of the door. A quick search of the pockets revealed a wallet and the set of keys I was looking for. There were several, all different sizes, and I chose two that might fit the outside door.

He murmured something incoherent, and I froze. You've been here before, I reminded myself, and if my memory served me correctly, it did not end well – for me. I had found out what the prison was hiding and had a sickening feeling that the place had more secrets to reveal. I wondered if he would be more settled in the bed, but I decided it would take too much time to move him.

The sedative, – if indeed that was what the prisoners had been receiving, would ensure he did not wake up. A quick check in the forbidden room would show me whether it was accessible, and one quick jab would give me a good window of opportunity. With trembling hands, I took the keys and tiptoed out of the room, pulling the door behind me.

Things have been going… okay, I told myself… This course of action had the potential to jeopardise everything. Whatever I uncovered in this room would alter everything; there would be no going back. I was surprised how easily the door opened and how ordinary the room looked. I pushed it as wide as it would go, and it bounced back slightly as it made contact with something behind it. Several coats hung on hooks. Like the cells, the room was approximately the size of a garage, and every wall was taken up with filing cabinets, cupboards or a door.

The door. The easy option would be to open it, lock it behind me and run as far as I could away from this place. But I couldn't. That wasn't the reason I had returned to the police station not so long ago. To escape now would defeat the whole purpose. I tried the door of the first cabinet, hoping it would be unlocked, but unsurprisingly it did not move. I could hear a faint rattle of glass inside. I systematically tried each key until I found the right one.

It appeared to be a medicine cabinet. Rows of vials and small jars filled the top shelf, and there were various first aid items: plasters, bandages, antiseptic wipes. I held up one of the vials, without the faintest idea what I was doing. The label was the same as I had seen in the file, the one routinely given to the prisoners. He'll wake up eventually with a sore arm and know what I've done, I told myself. I rubbed my arm, remembering how it had ached. Okay then, he'd know; but whatever happened from now on, this was the end. I decided to take two, in case one was not enough.

I stood over him, needle poised. Arm or leg? Which would ensure the drug entered his system quicker? This was the point of no return. All I had done so far was go into the room; I could easily lock it all up again and he'd be none the wiser. I did not come in here for nothing, I did not come in here for nothing, I repeated over and over again in my head, then I plunged the needle into his leg, epi-pen style. I hadn't factored in any movement from him, and panicked as his eyes shot open.

'Wha…' he mumbled groggily, as if disturbed from a deep sleep. Instinctively, I jumped on top of him, pinning down his arms. I felt him fighting, and he looked at me, eyes wide and confused. I smelled the whisky on his breath, and panted with the effort. Just inches away from his face, I watched as his eyes glassed over, then eventually closed. I regained my breath, as if I had fought a few rounds in a boxing match. When I was sure he was out for the count, I gingerly released my grip and climbed off him.

That should give me a few hours, I thought. I recalled the confusion when I had come around from sedation myself. I had probably been lying in that field for a good few hours. I checked my watch: 11.32. Plenty of time to look around. If he regained consciousness, I thought, maybe I could tell him I'd sedated him for his own good because I was worried for his safety… but somehow this didn't seem plausible. As I walked back to the previously locked room, what rang through my mind was *we killed them all, they're all dead*, and again I felt a chill run through me.

The second cupboard I opened was a large storage unit for food. Endless rows of packaged food and tins had been placed neatly on metal shelves. This surprised me, but also didn't. Of course I had not been living on cheese sandwiches while I had been on guard here. Joe had appeared regularly, armed with meals I could prepare myself and enough canned goods to keep me going for up to a week at a time. There was even a small kitchenette near my bedroom. Here there was every type of non-perishable food I could think of. Fruit and vegetables? No problem, there was a wide selection of tins. A person could live in here for years, I thought, then almost instantly, he's been doing just that. Even though he wasn't in a cell himself, this place had obviously affected his mental health. He could probably turn at any moment. This thought spurred me on; I was doing the right thing.

I came to the door, the way out. I discovered to my horror, that a metal keypad stood between it and my freedom. I randomly pressed a four-digit combination, with the faint hope that it would miraculously spring open. I could have spent a day pressing different codes and be no further forward. I put my hands behind my head for a moment, thinking, before lashing out and punching the door in frustration. There was still no way I could escape into the night, running as fast as my legs could carry me, far, far away from everything. I thought about the prisoners; any hopes I'd had of releasing every one was a fading dream. Even if I lowered the ladder into each cell, there was nowhere for them to go, and I potentially faced a mob of angry, insane convicts, furious at being detained in the first place, ready to seek vengeance on the nearest person. Judging by the video tapes, the shared mood was anger.

The next cupboard contained the most useful items. There were several firearms, and an old baseball bat. I picked up a gun, which felt heavy in my hands. The Chief was in the police force; these items were probably easy for him to obtain, or perhaps he had confiscated them from criminals. I took a few swings with the bat, finding it odd that it was in here too. It wasn't the weapon of choice if the going got tough, especially since there were guns as well.

The filing cabinet next to the weapons cupboard contained folders. This scared me even more, strangely enough, as I had an awful feeling that I wasn't going to like what was in them. All the same, I removed one and sat down to look at it.

The folder was large and the contents were separated by coloured dividers. The first section was labelled simply 'Prisoner 1'. This was the man responsible for the death of the Chief's daughter; I had been told the full story the day I arrived here. The file contained pictures of him and background information, arrest sheets and personal details. He used to live in the same town as I had. I peered at one of the entries: 'TTW', but couldn't work out what this could stand for. I put the folder on the table; I'd had enough of the acronyms and codes used in this place, and in any case I felt distanced from him. I did not know him and could not relate any of these details to him.

I instantly recognised the photo of 'Prisoner 2'. It was my dad. I had been shown the photos which were filed neatly in here; they had been taken undercover and showed his secret family. I allowed myself to study them in more detail now, and wondered what steps his girlfriend had taken once he had disappeared. Did she care, or did she think the same as my mum, that he had simply left and moved onto the next unsuspecting woman? I wondered if their relationship had been a happy one, or if she had been as miserable and dissatisfied as my mother.

The next page was handwritten, data organised into a table, showing dates and what appeared to be the sedative administered. I counted three separate occasions on when he had been drugged. I rubbed my head, confused. One of the dates seemed to coincide with my release from the prison just after I had broken into the Chief's house. I could not fathom what I was reading; had he been moved because of me? Then I realised – *the factory*. The place Chris and I had been led to by the Chief, the factory he had discovered us breaking into, the place where I had seen my father and no other prisoner. Had I been led to it deliberately, and been easy prey to capture? But in a bizarre twist, it was Chris they took and not me.

The pressure in my head was becoming overwhelming. Once my position here had been secured, I noted that he had been sedated again; *moved back here?* I sat still, feeling light-headed for a moment. Had he been used as lure to get me involved with all this? Of course the Chief had anticipated my moves, knew that I wouldn't just let things lie. He knew I would investigate and eventually go to the police. It looked as though *they* had been two steps ahead of me the whole time.

I aimlessly flicked through the next few sections of the file, not recognising anyone. They were all men, a similar age to my dad. One page stopped me in my tracks: staring me in the face was my own picture. I had been prisoner 5. I looked solemn, with nothing to smile about. My file contained nothing I didn't already know. My minor cautions from the police as a young teenager were recorded, and the date I had unsuspectingly broken into the Chief's house. I had been sedated twice, once on my arrival, when I could only assume I had been taken from my bed, and then again as they prepared me for my exit. Next to this was the date of my release. And then nothing, as though my file was closed: prisoner released and under surveillance.

I leaned back on the chair, mulling over how much of a challenge it was for them to drug people and transport them here. How easy was it to get them into the cell? Surely it must take more than two people? Maybe there were others involved that I wasn't aware of. Maybe there was someone else in the police force, aiding the Chief as he carried out his undercover duties. *I doubt you'll ever see him again*, began to play on a loop in my mind. I was annoyed that I hadn't seen any further newspapers to find out the identity of the dead policeman. Was it the Chief? Was that the reason I would never see him again? Frustrated, I flipped over the next sheet and instantly knew why this section of the file was so thin: it belonged to Chris.

There was no photograph as Chris was never on

their radar. There was no arrest sheet as Chris had always remained on the right side of the law. He'd even been a good student at school. It was a shame he had ever become involved in this. Hopefully, it was all a fading memory for him; perhaps he occasionally woke up after a nightmare, flopping back onto his pillow, gasping for breath and covered in sweat, realising he was safe, back home. I decided I would never contact him again; he wouldn't want any reminder of what I'd got him into. His file was very short, and handwritten. He'd been sedated once, I presumed on his arrival here.

I stared at this again. Sedated once? Surely this was not up to date; there was no entry for his release. Confused, I turned the page – nothing. The file just continued onto the next prisoner. I hastily leafed through it: a twenty-year-old, Anthony Turner. Back to Chris; why were his details not up to date? There was one final entry: 'TTW' again. This rang a bell; I had seen the code before. With bated breath, I flipped back to Prisoner 1, who had the same code. What did these two possibly have in common? Two men, from opposite ends of the criminal spectrum: what was the link?

I put my head in my hands. It was aching from all the new information I had absorbed in the last hour. I had a long night ahead and had begun to feel tired. With no natural daylight, my sense of night and day had begun to blur. I decided to check on Joe; he had not moved from the chair. I snapped my fingers a few times in front of his face to get his attention, quietly at first, but then louder. Then, I clapped once, before erupting into a succession of claps, a round of applause for no one. He didn't flinch; there was no response. I reached over to his glass and took a large swig of the contents. I was becoming used to this drink now; it seemed to give me the boost I needed.

My thoughts went back to the file – and all of a sudden I knew. The glass tumbled to my feet, the contents spilling and soaking into the carpet. I stood, frozen, as the awful realisation hit me. 'W' stood for well.

CHAPTER 29

My whole body was covered in a coating of sweat and felt hot and cold at the same time. My scalp prickled, and I stood stock still, afraid to move. 'TTW' – To The Well, Transferred To Well or Taken To Well. I recalled to my original visit to the surveillance room, when I first stared in horror at the images on the screens. I distinctly remembered being told that Prisoner 1 was in a well; I had been threatened with 'the well' before I was released. I still shuddered with fear at the thought of being thrown in this pit, denied any human contact whilst surviving in the ghastly conditions.

I stood in front of Prisoner one's screen. It was hard to make out his features as the image was so poor. There was no screen for Chris, naturally; his whole existence here was being shielded from me. I had been ignorant of my ignorance, carrying out my duties, none the wiser about how close he'd been the whole time. Of course he could never be released; *he knew too much*. He knew names and had seen locations. There was absolutely no way they could have allowed him to walk round with all that knowledge. He would have been like a ticking time bomb, and despite whatever promises he made, they would constantly be looking over their shoulders. They had put Chris into the well and used his 'release' as a lure to get me in here. I was under the illusion that he had been saved and I was doing them a favour. We were both prisoners in different ways.

Sitting back in the comfortable chair, I grabbed a pencil and the map of the cells. The cells had no writing on them so I noted the access cell and the supposedly empty cells I had been told about. Joe had informed me of the location of the cells. I had been providing food and drink to the metal grilles but had never once been spoken to, apart from Anthony. However, the empty trays had proved someone had been eating the provisions.

There seemed to be only one possible solution to this entire situation: get Chris out, and together we could decide what to do. I would convince him my being here was to save him, which in a way it was. I turned on all the lights, which still provided poor illumination for the underground corridors. The two wells were situated at the far end. It would be pure chance which one Chris was in. My finger hovered over the button to open the access hatch, but something made me pause. Surely it would make more sense for Chris to be in the one nearest to the other cells if Prisoner one was in the furthest well? I thought back to the map.

I hurried to the next well, took a deep breath and pressed the button hard. The hatch slid open with relative ease. The first thing to hit me was the overpowering stench. I turned away in disgust, coughing. Finding nothing in my pocket to use as a mask, I cupped my hand over my nose and mouth. It didn't work, so I held my nose and tried to breathe through my mouth. I crouched down and leaned over the mouth of the well. It was pitch dark, and I squinted, struggling to make out anything at all.

There was a light switch next to the release button.

I pressed it quickly, and turned on a dim lightbulb. I edged closer to the entrance, half expecting some mutant half-human to spring out at me. I told myself this was ridiculous, and resigned myself to the fact that the reality of who was down there and the condition they were in was more frightening than any fiction my imagination could conjure up.

He sat, curled in a ball, head bowed. His shirt, once a smart blue denim, had turned brownish. His hair, normally carefully washed and styled, stood out in all directions.

'Chris...' I whispered.

He lifted his head to look at me. His eyes were puffy and his face was smeared with dirt. A small spark of life lit his face as he croaked, 'Jim? Thank God. I knew you'd come back.'

I breathed a massive sigh of relief and let out a choked gasp. It was like being reunited with a long-lost relative after several years. The putrid air was now forgotten.

'Thank God you're... alive,' I half-sobbed. 'I'm going to get you out of there.'

'No, Jim, the guy here, he's crazy...' He stretched out his hand towards me, his tone almost frantic. 'You've no idea some of the things he's been saying... about you...'

'I can well imagine, but we're okay for the moment. I'm... we're all locked up in here too, but at least I can get you out of there and up here. Anything is better than down there.'

'Okay, okay.' He nodded rapidly using the wall as a prop to stand. The well was much smaller than the cell I'd been in; at best it measured about six feet or so in diameter. For a tall person, this would be torture enough, not being able to lie flat.

'I'll lower the ladder,' I told him, and positioned it carefully, using both hands to slide it over. It wobbled slightly, making me gasp. I composed myself, adjusted my grip and started again. The alcohol, the adrenaline, the excitement at the prospect of saving Chris and having a kindred spirit to plot an escape from this place made me tremble. This was the best feeling I'd had in a long time; finally I was saving someone's life.

'Be careful,' I panted as the bottom of the ladder reached his outstretched hands. I smiled, relieved, as he took hold of it. His eyes met mine, and I imagine for the first time in weeks he smiled too.

'You have the police with you?' he asked. He had already positioned the ladder and tested that it was resting securely against the wall.

'Not exactly, but we'll talk more when you're out.'

I didn't notice the smell as he began his climb. It didn't matter; he was my friend, and I'd soon be able to fix him up with a warm shower, clean clothes and a proper meal as we discussed our next steps. He looked down and quickly back at me as he climbed, his smile becoming wider. I returned his smile – it was though we were children again, happy to see each other after a long absence. I was now inches from him, and reached out my hand, almost able to make contact with him. I felt his fingers brush against the tips of mine.

'Oh!' He took in a sharp breath as he lost his footing. Panic was etched on his face as he plunged back down, twice as fast as he'd climbed.

'Chris!' I shouted, as if my cry could assist him in any way. 'Chris!' My voice cracked. I could see one of his shoes at the bottom of the well. No shoelaces.

His grip had tightened on the sides of the ladder, and as he slid down I imagined numerous splinters embedding themselves in his palms. He came to a sudden stop on one of the bottom rungs, then I heard a sharp snap as the rung broke. He staggered backwards, arms flailing wildly, and the ladder whipped out of my grasp. I could only watch, appalled, as his head collided with the wall with a dull, sickening thud and he sank almost gracefully to the floor.

Silence. My arm remained outstretched, in some vain attempt to catch him, frozen with panic. The ladder jutted at a strange angle, too far away from the hatch to be of use to either of us. Chris sat in almost the same position as I had found him, except now he looked like a discarded marionette, slumped at an angle, head bowed, eyes closed. I imagined a pool of blood slowly spreading across the floor of the well.

'Chris! Chris!' I shouted until my lungs ached, as if there was a chance I could rouse him. It was useless. His head had hit the brick wall with crushing force. He was dead, and I cried great heaving sobs as a heavy pain formed in my chest. My fingers felt the lip of the brickwork, and I lowered my head and howled. I cried for my dead friend, for all the horrible, twisted events which had unfolded in the last few months, for my dad, for the other desperate prisoners, and for the cold, dark, unforgiving walls of this place.

I remained there for some time, unable and afraid to move, not wanting to accept that there was nothing else I could do for Chris. I didn't know how long I lay there, my gaze fixed on him. My best friend was dead, and I had killed him.

I wiped my eyes with the back of my hand, smearing dirt across my face. My feet were heavy, and I felt like someone with all the world's troubles on his shoulders. I walked on autopilot back to the secret room, opened the weapons cupboard, and took out the baseball bat and a gun.

CHAPTER 30

D*ear Dad,*

This is an extremely difficult letter for me to write as there is nothing that I can do to save you. I'm afraid that I can't speak to you to tell you this as that would be too hard. I have been watching and looking after you for some time now. This has been my punishment for the crimes I have committed: to watch you and not be able to get you out. I have been overseeing this prison for some time, but I am locked in here myself. The exit has a code which I don't know, and I don't know if I'll ever be able to get it.

I was hoping I could see you properly again. There was only one ladder for all of the cells but sadly this is now destroyed and I am not able to reach it to try and mend it.

I just wanted to say that I know about everything you've done. I know about your girlfriend and your children. I know why you are in here too. You witnessed a girl being murdered and then gave a false alibi for her killer. I am in here because I happened to break into her house.

I don't know if either of us will make it out of here alive. Whatever happens from here on, I just wish things had been better

between us on the outside.
      Your son, James

I re-read my letter several times. Other drafts were littered around my feet like the aftermath of a snowball fight. My hand hovered over the page; I was half tempted to scrunch this version into a tight ball and toss it to join the others, but I paused and decided to leave it for the moment. When I had a draft I was satisfied with, I planned to slip it under his plate at the next mealtime.

I sat opposite Joe, waiting for the slightest movement. I had showered and changed my clothes, but not before I had searched every cupboard in the storage unit. There was nothing else, no clue to the code to get out of here. I had found some surgical tape, which I used to secure Joe's hands and legs to the chair. Now I sat looking at him, waiting for him to wake up. I had no real idea of my plans when he did. Either he would die or we both would. If I had the upper hand, I would force the code for the door out of him in whatever way necessary.

His breathing faltered momentarily, and I sat up, straight and alert. But he continued to sleep. I wondered how much I actually knew about this man. I had no knowledge of his life outside this prison, where he went after he left me in charge. He didn't wear a wedding ring, but I couldn't be certain whether he had a family.

One thing I was certain of was that I was being used; I was never some kind of protégé, being trained to run the whole unit single-handedly. He and the Chief probably met every night, having a laugh at how easily they had managed to dupe me. But no more. This was the end.

My eyes grew heavy and I allowed them to close now and again, but every time my head lolled, I jerked upright again. I didn't want to sleep and have Chris's image in my head haunting my dreams. I must have dozed, though; I woke up abruptly to the sound of murmuring from the chair opposite.

His hands pushed against the restraints and he shook his head to clear his eyes. I had used two whole rolls of the surgical tape to ensure his hands were tightly bound. He tried to pull free, and his fingers flexed wide, then he relaxed and his eyes met mine. The second syringe of sedative lay on the desk between us.

'James.' He was almost smiling at me, as though he'd been expecting this to happen one day. 'Just what are you planning?'

I regarded him and said nothing for a few moments, mimicking the way he had irritated me so many times. Then I said, 'We're going to talk, or rather, I'm going to ask some questions and you're going to answer them. Simple as that.'

'And if I don't?' He had spied the bat on my lap.

I grasped the handle and held it tightly. 'It's probably best if you do.' I stood up and began to push the table. I didn't want a barrier between us. It was heavy, and it was soon clear I wouldn't be able to move it singlehandedly, so I resorted to lifting one end and pivoting it; one end prevented the door from opening fully, but it didn't matter as I didn't envisage needing a quick exit.

'And the restraints?' He pulled at them with his hands. 'You think this is completely necessary?'

'I think you're very dangerous,' I replied. 'So yes, I do think they are necessary.'

'Despite what you might think, I've never killed anyone.'

'And you're sure about that?' I was growing angry at his continuing arrogance. 'I distinctly recall you telling me how your first attempt at a prison had ended with everyone dead. You told me you'd killed them all...'

He cut me off, almost laughing. 'James, you have no idea. You've got it all wrong...'

'Then you tell me how I'm supposed to interpret a

statement like that?' I was really angry now, and felt the need to stand up and pace around. Besides, if I stood over him, it might give me an air of authority.

'I said we'd killed them, but I meant by accident. Haven't you ever done anything by accident?'

My thoughts instantly flashed back to Chris. Yes that had been a tragic accident, but surely there was no comparison.

He must have seen something in my face. 'It was a chemical leak, I think,' he said. 'We never really did find out the cause, but yes, under our care they were poisoned in some way. It was never our intention. I did tell you we're not murderers James, and I meant that.'

'What right do you have?' I turned away from him in disgust. 'To decide what is wrong, and how people should be punished?'

'I've already explained, conventional prison is not working. This place, our intentions… what other solution would you have for repeat offenders?'

'Rehabilitation,' I replied. 'People can be rehabilitated…'

'Rehabilitation.' He sounded disgusted. 'It doesn't work James, and it's an extra expense, in an already overworked system.'

'It's not your place to decide!' I shouted at him.

He sighed. 'Have you ever lost anyone? I mean, someone you really cared about?' I saw in his face that this was personal to him, so I let him continue. 'I have. I lost my whole family, my goddaughter Emily and a woman…' He paused and swallowed hard. 'A woman I cared very deeply for. They were all murdered, in one way or another. The people to blame all spent time in prison, were released and then what? It became very clear that they had not learnt their lesson.' He chewed on his bottom lip, and if his hands were free, he would probably have his head in them. Tears formed in his eyes, and for a moment, I could almost empathise with him.

'There are people in here who are nothing to do with you or the Chief.' I wasn't just referring to Chris. I wondered if he realised I'd found him.

He inhaled deeply. 'There's a pattern,' he said. 'Kids seem to start with minor crimes, then they escalate. The Chief sees it all the time in his job. All we're doing is pre-empting the crimes they will go onto commit.'

I sat down again, slightly more composed. 'You can't lock someone up for something they might do,' I said. I didn't want to mention Chris; it was still too raw. But I wasn't sure how things were going to progress.

He shifted in his seat, and flexed his hands again. 'Don't you see that about your dad's case? His testimony could have put a man behind bars, but he lied and allowed that man to walk free. And he has a long record himself.' I chewed at my thumbnail, uncomfortable now. 'No more hurt James,' he added. 'He can't hurt you any more while he's here.'

We both fell silent. I didn't know how to respond. Maybe he was right. I decided to keep him talking.

'You asked me if I'd ever lost someone. Okay, I have.'

'Tell me about it.'

'I watched someone I care about a lot, a very good friend, die in front of me. It wasn't long ago.' My throat thickened and I cleared it.

'How did it happen?' he asked. 'Was it an accident, or was someone at fault?'

'It was someone's fault. Someone is to blame. You could say he was murdered. A victim of circumstance, if you will.'

'Then I'm sure you want that person to pay,' he said bitterly. I could tell he was thinking that we'd finally found common ground, after he'd battled to get me on his side and make me see things his way.

'I want that person to pay very much,' I replied.

He smiled. 'Then you'll release me?' he asked

softly, testing me. I did not move. His eyes broke contact with mine and his lips twitched as if he wanted to laugh. I replayed the conversation in my mind. I hadn't seen the penny-drop moment, the moment that he figured out what I knew. How clever he was, playing me all that time.

'You've done well,' he said nonchalantly.

I frowned at him, confused.

He went on, 'you've been in here alone, all this time and you haven't snooped, put your nose in what is forbidden. Who have you talked to, besides your dad?'

'I haven't talked to him,' I shot back. 'Not once. Is that why you told me never to press the button? You didn't want me talking to him?'

'I didn't want you talking to any of the prisoners. They don't deserve that.'

I vowed never to tell him about my conversation with Anthony. I didn't want to tell him the real reason why I had never pressed the button: I'd just been too afraid. I couldn't bear the prospect of listening to my father beg me for something that I couldn't give him, and the last thing I wanted was for him to get out while I was here. As for the other inmates, there was nothing I could offer them either. Perhaps I could give them *him*, but then they would naturally assume I was in on the scheme as well.

I was fed up of all of the mind games. 'Tell me why you took Chris, and why he is still here. That's one huge lie you can't talk your way out of.'

His hands lay still now. 'We brought him here the night you went into the old factory.' Had he realised there was no point in lying any more? 'Why is he still here? Because he has seen our faces, has seen places, simple as that. There is no way we could risk him being outside with that knowledge.'

'Then you used him to get me in here.'

'Interpret that how you want. You also know too much James. It's lucky for us that you went to the people you did…'

I stood up slowly, grasping the handle of the baseball bat. My palm felt sweaty, and I adjusted my grip. He didn't flinch; it was as though he was expecting me to strike. I rested the bat on the empty chair and looked at it, then back at him. I wanted him to be afraid of me as I had been of him. I gathered my courage and walked to him, reaching out with the bat so it touched his face. I gently ran it down his cheek, almost caressing him.

'You'll tell me the code to get out of here,' I said flatly.

'You know I can't do that.' He did flinch slightly now.

I turned suddenly and smashed the bat down on the table. He jumped and gasped. The impact reverberated up my arm.

'I said, you'll tell me the code!' I shouted. The bat had made a small dent in the surface of the desk. 'Tell me, or the next time I swing this, I'll be more accurate.' I pointed it at his head.

He took a sharp breath as the bat made contact with his face again. There it was – what I'd been waiting for, the fear.

'How many people do you work for?' I decided to change tack, thinking about what I would do when I got out. He let out a nervous laugh.

'How many people do I work for?' he repeated. 'You think you've stumbled on a mass conspiracy? Sorry to disappoint you, but it's just me and the Chief, although we do have people on the outside, doing us favours...'

'I think you're afraid of him,' I teased. 'Otherwise, why are you here? I mean, what sane person would *volunteer* to be here, twenty-four-seven? I think you're a nobody on the outside; he's the one with the good job, and you're nothing. Being here makes you feel important. Am I right?' He did not respond, but something in his expression told me I had hit a raw nerve.

'I think there's more to this than you're telling me.

You said the man in the cell murdered Emily, but why do you keep such a close guard on something that is personal to the Chief? What has he got on you?'

I raised the bat again and he shied away. 'You've no idea what you're talking about,'

'What is it, are you secretly Emily's real father?' He didn't react. 'Or were you in love with his wife?' I threw this in, a wild stab in the dark, but the poker face he was trying so hard to sustain slipped ever so slightly.

'That's it, isn't it?' I mocked. 'You secretly loved his wife. That explains her picture in your room, before you cleared it out. And you've just told me that you lost a woman you cared for very deeply. So he made you stay in here as punishment when he found out. Then she killed herself. Why was that? Because she couldn't decide which of you to choose?' I smiled, pleased at having worked out the story behind this place and he must have thought I was making fun of his feelings.

'Shut up!' he roared. 'You've no idea what you're talking about!'

I leaned closer to whisper. 'But I'm right, aren't I? Get us out of here, and I'll help you get your revenge on him.'

He snorted and turned his head away. But I'd got under his skin now. 'Tell me the code,' I repeated again. 'Tell me now.'

'No!' he resisted. 'Go to hell!'

I moved the bat to within an inch of his face, anger bubbling up inside me. I would need something more than this to make him realise that I meant business. All my life I had been put down by someone: first my father, and now the Chief, and him, this man in front of me. But no more. I needed to stand up for myself for once.

'You do what you need to do,' he said, almost daring me to do something. 'What is the use of living a life if you have no life to live?' His eyes drifted away, and I wasn't sure if he was talking about himself or me. What had he sacrificed to be in here? How much did he know about me?

'This is your last chance,' I said. 'Tell me the code for the door. I'll leave right now and you won't ever see me again.'

Our eyes locked, neither of us willing to give way. I was still poised, bat in hand, and my other hand gripped the handle. Suddenly, two-handed, I brought the bat down on his knee, all my anger focused in the blow. His yell of pain rang out across the room. If I had been able to see sound waves, I was sure they would have rippled outwards, like throwing a pebble into a lake. He jerked violently in his seat, unable to draw his legs up to defend himself from further attack. All he could do was struggle against the tape and writhe around in agony. I watched him, giving away no emotion, but regretting having to hurt him.

His cries subsided, and his leg still twitched with pain. Every time he tried to move it, he took a sharp breath. His smart trousers were close fitting, and I saw a swelling start to form. He leaned back as far as the chair would allow and closed his eyes.

'I should have kept you in the cell, or put you back in when I had the chance...' he muttered.

'But you didn't. And now you will sit there until you are ready to talk.' I took a final look at him, then turned around and headed out of the door.

CHAPTER 31

It hit me as I sat in the comfortable leather chair again, and I began to shake. I had probably shattered the kneecap of a defenceless man, and I had done it on purpose in order to get some information out of him. And for what? I was no further forward, he hadn't told me what I needed to know. I hardly recognised myself.

But he had pushed me, lied to me about Chris being released. They never had any intention of letting him go. My regrets began to dissolve as I remembered why I was so full of rage; he, they, this set-up had killed my friend. They had probably heaved a huge sigh of relief the day I walked into the police station, straight into the path of the Chief. But didn't Joe say that others had been released, or was that a lie too? Were there others walking around free, scared into being model citizens?

All he had given me was his reaction when I quizzed him about holding a torch for the Chief's late wife. I strode out of the room towards the supply room, retrieved the file on the prisoners and thumbed through it to Prisoner one's details. This was the man who had murdered Emily. There were several pictures of him, and his arrest sheet and several newspaper cuttings following the trial. This was someone my father obviously knew, as he had provided an alibi for him.

I leafed through the newspaper stories, and the sorry headlines stood out: 'Hunt for missing girl continues'. This told how Emily had not returned home following a night out on her eighteenth birthday. 'Grim discovery in hunt for missing girl' described how her disappearance was being treated as murder after her body was found by a dog walker. She was a pretty girl and was pictured with her parents before the tragedy occurred. I couldn't identify either David or Joe's features in her; she looked like her mother. There were other clippings covering her killer's trial, and one final story about Jill driving her car into a river.

I paused and breathed deeply, putting the folder down. It had not made pleasant reading, and for an instant I could understand the Chief's desire for vengeance. I just didn't want to be caught up in the middle of it. I resented the fact that it was now down to me to keep the killer alive. His arrest sheet concluded with Jill's death, even though he was not directly responsible. Had she killed herself through grief or because of the love triangle? I stared at their personal details; Emily had not been much older than me, and a quick calculation told me that Jill had had her relatively young.

'Oh my God,' I muttered. I looked at the door, my escape route from this place. Could it be that simple? I strode over to it, and with a trembling hand, input Emily's date of birth into the keypad. The door remained locked.

'Come on, come on…' I whispered, willing the door to open. I paused, then decided to try Jill's date of birth. The door gave a click, and I let out a laugh as I pushed it open. The breeze seemed to welcome me, and I allowed myself to take several large gulps of fresh air. I began to well up as all the pent-up tension struggled to get out. I felt like an explorer who had been stuck in a cave for weeks.

Using the folder to prop the door open, I took a step outside. I could hardly believe my eyes – I was in the exact same place the Chief had sent me. So near to everything familiar. Inside, I could have been a hundred miles away from home, or just ten.

I carefully pulled the door so that it rested against the folder. Even though I knew the code, I dared not close it fully. Back in the small office, I saw Joe, still in the same position. His eyes snapped open when I went back in.

Repeated pulling against the tape had slackened it noticeably; I reckoned I had less than an hour before he freed himself. His leg still jutted out in front of him; he might free his hands, but there was no way he would be able to run after me. This should give me a good solid lead before he raised the alarm or the Chief came looking for him.

'I'll be off now,' was all I could think of to say.

'Oh James,' he called. I turned to face him. 'Just watch your back, that's all.'

I sneered. 'You and your empty threats...' I waited for a few seconds, wanting some kind of reaction from him. I wanted him to beg me to release him, tell me he was sorry for everything that had happened. There was nothing. I picked up the other syringe of sedative, maintaining eye contact with him. As I stood over him and saw a small flicker in his eyes. That was it – the look I had been waiting for. Fear.

'I wanted you to know what it feels like,' I whispered. 'Everything you've put me through...' I plunged the needle into his arm and threw it across the room. I wondered fleetingly if there would be any side effects after two doses, and watched as he slipped into unconsciousness.

I quickly loosened the tape on his hands, pulled him out of the chair and laid him flat on the floor.

Dragging him was hard, and it took several attempts to get him round the desk and out of the door. I knew exactly where I was heading; he could wake up in the horrific well he had forced Chris to stay in. I sprinted back up the stairs into the bedroom area, and found spare bedsheets. The crude hoist I fashioned would have to do; I didn't have long. I lowered Joe into the well, and gave him a final look as he lay half over Chris's body. How I wished I could be here when he woke up.

Back in the bedroom I stuffed a few clothes into my bag. I had already emptied Joe's wallet; the cash would help a little. I decided to pack one of the handguns from the storage room. I hated guns and didn't want to be caught with it but I felt I needed to take it.

The letter I had written to my dad lay on the desk. I mulled over what to do with it, checking my watch. It would soon be morning and I had to get out. But who would feed the prisoners, and when would they be discovered? There was no way I could release every single one even if I wanted to. I took tins from the food cupboard and stacked as many as would fit on each tray. This would keep them going until I could raise the alarm. It didn't take long to deliver each one in through the grille.

I paused at the grille leading into my dad's cell, the letter in my hand. There was no way I could get him out. Significant moments in my life before all this flashed through my mind, like scenes on a storyboard. Memories I didn't want to relive sprang into my mind. This man had truly been a terrible father to me, a terrible husband to my mother. The image of Sally slowly dissolved in my head. Yes, he had been an awful role model, and perhaps he deserved to be where he was. I took a few moments to mull over the letter again before slipping it on his tray under one of the tins.

My final act before leaving the cell area was to switch on every light. I told myself they might feel slightly more human if they could see. I also wanted Joe to wake and see exactly where he was.

Back in the secret room, I quickly looked round in case I'd missed anything. Inconspicuously behind the door was *that* bag again. I hadn't seen it before; as the door had hidden it. It must have been what had prevented it from opening fully. I ran my fingers over the italic letters – D.F. He had been so particular about wanting this back. I had stupidly not broken into it before, but I wasn't letting it get away from me again; it obviously contained something of great importance. I would take great pleasure in forcing the lock open. But not here. I put the prisoner file in my own bag and picked both up. Then I shut the door behind me and walked away.

The morning sun peeped through the warehouses, giving the sky a warm orange glow. For everyone else this was just an ordinary sunrise, but for me it felt different. I couldn't bring myself to smile just yet; my insides were still churning and the sense of foreboding doom still lingered.

The sound of my footsteps bounced off the walls. It had been a while since I had walked any distance and I was surprised to feel my legs ache after only a short time. I looked down at my shoes; this time the laces were intact. I turned a corner and noticed that the street was deserted; I was in the middle of nowhere. I adjusted my grip on the bags, often changing hands. After a short time, I realised something wasn't right. The smell hit me first, thick and heavy, as if a firework had gone off. Then there was smoke, puffing round my hand. Confusion hit me – why was this happening now and hadn't happened before when I first stole the bag? I smiled triumphantly – they had finally realised it was game over and I had won. They had detonated the bag knowing that there was no way that they'd ever get it back now.

I gasped fearing what might happen next and dropped the Chief's leather bag, then ran back to the corner. I crouched, hands over my ears, waiting for the explosion. Seconds passed, but nothing happened. After a few minutes I dared to peek around the corner, expecting billows of smoke and a crackling fire.

But the smoke had disappeared and the bag lay where I had left it. There was no fire. I moved carefully towards it and gingerly moved it with my foot, but nothing happened. The pungent smell still lingered, and it hit me that I knew exactly what had happened. I was right, it was a security device. Being my father's son had exposed me to things that I should not have witnessed or heard. I recalled a conversation between my father and my uncle Robin, about someone who had held up a security officer as he was walking to his van. He had threatened him with a gun, and made off with a large cash box. Opening the box had triggered the security device which emitted smoke, and the smell lingered on him for days. My father and uncle had found this highly amusing.

That's why he checked your hands, a small voice in my head told me. When I first met Joe, which seemed like years ago now, he'd asked to see my hands. Sometimes they fit dye in those bags too, I heard my father say. Same idea; the dye covers the contents and is very difficult to wash off… I had a sick feeling that my decision about whether to break into the bag had been a factor in whether or not to release me from the cell. I didn't open the bag, so they probably would have let me go. Had all of this been for nothing? Would they have left me alone as long as I behaved? No. Now I was aware of their covert prison, the implications were enormous. If I exposed them it would mean the end of the Chief's career as well as prison sentences for him and Joe.

But I hadn't tried to open it. The lock was still intact. Something had activated the security device. I shuddered, nausea rising inside me, now replaced the smug feeling I'd had a few moments ago. Someone must have triggered it. Joe? Impossible, he was stuck in the well. It didn't make sense though – I'd had the bag before and nothing had happened. I began to walk briskly away, half convinced Joe would come running around the corner, or worse, the Chief might turn up to do a morning check, two takeaway coffees in hand. I pictured Joe, in agony, screaming from the well, cursing my name as the Chief fumbled in his pocket for the trigger to set off the bag. I had no idea if any of this was possible; I just had to get away, even though I was still desperate to find out what the bag contained. I took a few steps, then stopped. Everything that had happened – this bag was at the centre of it. I couldn't just leave it.

Rubbing my forehead, I turned back. A quick look round told me I was alone. For Christ's sake, just make a decision! I scolded myself. The clock is ticking, you've not got much time. Impulsively I pulled the bag into the doorway of a disused office block. You may have less than half an hour, I told myself, frantically searching my own bag for something to break the lock. I found nothing – then I gasped as I remembered the prisoner file. There was a metal bar inside, securing the pages. It would have to do.

Firstly, I tried to force the bag open with my bare hands, hoping that the lock would give with a small amount of force, but I knew this wouldn't work. With shaking hands, I placed the metal bar under the padlock and tried to prise it off. The leather around the lock stretched tight. A few further attempts stretched it further, and as I moved the metal bar back and forth, the leather slackened. Come on, come on, I willed it, trying hard not to think about the time I was spending on this. I glanced around once more, then concentrated on the job in hand. *You will open, you will open, you will…*

Open.

The mechanism snapped and I narrowly missed slicing my hand on the jagged edge. I tossed the metal bar aside and took another anxious look up the street, half expecting Joe or the Chief to charge towards me, screaming. But as before, nothing. With the same delicacy I imagined a bomb disposal expert would use on an unexploded device, I lifted the leather strap.

The first thing I saw was an inky plastic sachet at the top of the bag. I took a sharp breath; this was the second security device, and for some reason it had failed to detonate. There was still a strong smell of smoke, but that was all. The contents of the bag were intact and untainted. I grasped a handful of papers from the bag carefully manoeuvring them under the bag of dye, and repeated the process until I had emptied it. I now had a stack of papers a few inches tall. A breeze ruffled the top sheet so I rested my knee on it.

I quickly leafed through the papers, randomly absorbing words, sentences, phrases. *Prisoner number one details... purchase of warehouse... surveillance notes...* the information soon became a blur. My time was running out; I needed to move. I unzipped my own bag and dumped all of the paperwork into it. There was no way I wanted to take the Chief's bag, so I pushed it into a corner, then stood up and began walking away.

I slowed down momentarily as something occurred to me. I had leafed through the ring binder at the prison, but had no opportunity to read it thoroughly. I tried hard to recall if I had seen either the Chief's name or Joe's. Was there anything in there to link the two of them to the prisoners? Did the contents of the Chief's bag fill any gaps? I hoped I would find something in one or the other to implicate them both.

I walked a mile or so before I reached a main road, and I picked up the pace, eager to see some other signs of life. A taxi pulled up, its lights still on despite the fact that it was now daylight. It was the most welcoming piece of normality I had seen in a long while.

I nervously tapped on the side window. 'Are you free?'

The driver looked up from his paper and rolled down his window. 'Just finished an airport run.' I gratefully slid into the back.

'You're out early,' he commented as he pulled away.

'It's a long story.' I leant back, sinking into the seat.

'Say no more,' he replied. 'You have my sympathy though'

'Hmm?'

'Being stuck out here, alone. The day before I was due to get married, I was abandoned by so-called friends in nothing but a pink tutu in the middle of nowhere, I kid you not!' he chortled.

I smiled at the ordinariness of the conversation. Part of me craved silence, but I didn't want to be alone with my thoughts, and welcomed his mindless chatter.

He went on, 'similar thing happened to my stepson not so long ago.'

'What was that?' I asked.

'Being abandoned. He was out one night with friends, and swore his drink was spiked or something. Said he woke up in a strange room. He wouldn't say much about it. Wouldn't go to the police or anything. Embarrassed, I suppose.'

I froze, a little sickened but also intrigued. 'So what happened?' I managed to ask.

'Like I say, he wouldn't say much, but it put the fear of God into him. He'd always been a bit of a handful, not a bad kid but mixed with the wrong type, you know the sort.' I was sure the colour was draining from my face. 'Scared him straight in some way. He enrolled for an apprenticeship and that's been him ever since. I'd even go so far as to say we're proud of him, the way he's turned things around.'

The morning traffic began to build and he stopped talking. I didn't want to dwell on the implications of what he had said.

'Where are you heading?' he asked

I looked out of the window. 'I'm not sure,' I

replied. 'Keep on going out of town please. Head north.'

He did as I asked and we sat in silence. I didn't want to know any more about his stepson. I stared out the window, struggling to take in the vast expanse of the outside. We began to slow down, as a queue of traffic snaked back from a crossroads, and panic rose inside me. I wanted to keep moving, the further away from that place, the better. Glancing to my left, I saw a large, white building with a sign that read Community College. I thought back to Craig, working hard on his studies. Was this where he was enrolled? One of my options could be to track him down. I had no idea what I would do if I did, but at least it would be someone to share my awful experience with. Maybe we could discuss the next steps; we could approach a police force a few counties away, so not to run into the Chief again. I drew my bag closer to me, protecting the precious information inside. I had evidence this time; I could make several copies, and distribute them to senior law enforcement and my local MP. Surely they would be able to piece it all together, and arrest David and Joe. I began to fantasise: as soon as every prisoner was out, I would drop a match and burn the prison to the ground, leaving David and Joe beating the walls, fighting to get out.

It was dangerous to stay in town though. This was *their* town. They could easily track me down again. *Watch your back...* I had to keep heading out of town, as far as Joe's money would allow, then plot my next steps somewhere new. This would buy me some time; I could look further into what was in the files, use the internet. I potentially had someone to help me, what was his name? Isaac? Isaac Watkins? I'd plan my revenge from a safe distance.

Most of the traffic was heading straight ahead. A lorry was stationary in what was probably a yellow box junction, preventing cars from getting past. On the other side of it was a new life for me, a new start. I could forget about it all, abandon the file; the Chief would go in search of Joe before too long, and they would sort out the prisoners, silently cursing at me as being the one who got away. I would meet a nice girl, settle down and look for a good job. We would be happy.

The driver drummed the wheel with his fingers and tutted loudly. 'It's the same every morning here. I swear the timings of these lights are wrong. I can go a different way if you still want to get out of town. You'll get to where you want to be eventually.' He shifted in his seat and turned round to face me.

'So what do you want to do?'

I stared out of the window, fear starting to mount up inside me. My options seemed overwhelming, and I started to feel light-headed.

'Hey?' the taxi driver said gently. 'Are you okay?'

I couldn't seem to form any words. My shoulders began to shake as the tears flowed. All the emotion I had been suppressing came flooding to the surface. I was a bad person, Joe had said it a while ago, it was in my blood, but I desperately wanted to be different. Uncontrollable sobs racked through me, and I put my head in my hands, tears soaking into my sleeves.

A car horn behind us beeped impatiently. In his concern, the driver hadn't seen the lights change. He moved off, still throwing anxious looks at me when he had the chance. He turned a sharp right and the traffic diminished; perhaps he was afraid I would jump out if we were stationary, and land in the path of oncoming cars. He pulled into the car park of a shopping mall and stopped at the end furthest from the shops. At this time of the morning, the place was deserted.

'Kid, are you okay?' he asked me again. He sounded fatherly, and it was the nicest anyone had been to me in a long while.

I looked up at him, rocking slightly to help me calm down. My eyes felt gritty and puffy, a combination of lack of sleep and heavy crying. I fixed my gaze on a plaque on the door, afraid to meet his eyes.

'I've done a bad thing.' My voice was barely above a whisper. 'Everything is my fault. I started it all.'

He checked his watch and looked back at me. 'Look, I've finished my shift. I can't let you get out, not in this state…'

'He was right, I am a bad person, but he can't get away with it, they can't get away with it…' I was rambling, random thoughts spilling out.

'Tell me,' the driver pressed. 'Nothing is as bad as it seems. I've always been told I'm a good listener.'

I looked up at him: greying hair and a weathered face. His fingers were curled around the edge of the screen opening, as if he was inviting me to take his hand if I needed to. He wore a plain gold wedding ring. The words poured out of me as I recounted every detail I could remember of the last few months. The story could have been lifted straight out of a crime novel yet every part was true; I didn't need to exaggerate at all. The secret prison set up because of the Chief's daughter; how he had convinced Joe to join with him to become underground prison wardens with their own agenda; my dad's involvement, and how I stupidly broke into the Chief's house and stole the one item that would bring their whole world crashing down like a house of cards.

As I described the horrors of the prison, his expression changed and his eyes widened like saucers.

'I want to change,' I concluded. 'After everything that's happened, I've learnt my lesson. They've won in that way, I'll do anything to never end up back there. They've done what they set out to do to me. That's it now; I'm disappearing, starting over, they'll hear no more from me…'

'You said you had evidence. If everything you've said is true then…'

'They'll find me though, track me down and throw

me back in there. Or kill me…' I choked back more tears.

'Not if you do it properly,' he urged, 'give everything you've got to the most senior policeman you can find. And I'm sure the papers would have a field day.'

'I can't.' I was shaking at the mere thought of going back to the police again.

'Then give it all to me. I'll do it. Give them to me, James, I'll…'

Suddenly I was no longer listening to him. It was as though an alarm had gone off in my head.

'How do you know my name?' I snapped.

'You told…' he stuttered.

'How do you know my name!' I shouted.

'You told me, just before…'

I searched frantically around the back of the taxi. Joe had mentioned that they had people working for them on the outside. Everyone was in on this. Soon a car would screech into the car park. A hidden microphone had picked up our entire conversation. The fact that he had pulled into an empty place gave the tracking device a chance to do its work. I couldn't believe I had been so naïve. The plaque on the door even spelled it out in black and white: licensed taxi driver – Jerry Foster. Foster… He was in on it too…

I threw the door open and launched myself onto the tarmac. Everything slowed down as I landed awkwardly, but ignoring the pain in my arm I scrambled to my feet and started to run. I heard him calling, his shouts fading away as I put some distance between us. Colours blurred in front of me, moving vehicles blended into the shop fronts as I approached the main road. Get away from him, far away before he could catch me, pin me to the ground, waiting for the Chief to come and take me back. I would spend the rest of my life rotting away in a purpose-built cell.

The screech of the brakes stopped me dead, and my world went into slow motion. The impact must have been hard as I landed several feet away from the van. My legs felt as though they were no longer part of me, and my head hit the road with a painful thud. I barely registered the people around me but felt firm hands on both my arms.

A jumble of voices: 'Don't try to get up… don't move… the ambulance is on its way… you'll be fine…'

Everything turned grey, like the cell walls, as I sank into unconsciousness.

***

I was just about able to make out the hazy shape on the wall as I lay, slowly emerging from what had felt like a very heavy sleep. The mattress I lay on felt soft, and an antiseptic aroma prickled my nose. My throat felt dry as I tried to speak, and nothing came out at first.

'Where am I?' I heard myself mumble, in a voice which did sound like mine. I blinked to allow for my eyes to become accustomed to the light. I made out a television on the wall, facing my bed. A man I did not recognise was watching it intently.

'Welcome back.' A nurse appeared in my line of sight. 'We were wondering when you'd wake up.' She turned to face the man on the chair. 'We need to run some tests, but you can have a few minutes.'

He slowly turned to face me and edged closer.

'You were in a nasty accident, but you'll be fine, *Nathan*, just fine.' He spoke this name clearly, almost as a signal for me not to question him. I didn't need to stutter to him that he'd called me by the wrong name. I watched as he scratched the side of his head and his wedding ring gleamed at me.

'Just fine…' His voice petered out and he signalled for me to watch the television. The news on the hour summarised the main stories. Dominating the headlines was a familiar name. David Foster, Chief Inspector at

Crenley Hampton, a town several miles away, had been exposed as a corrupt policeman who had used his position to set up his own covert prison. He had reportedly died from a self-inflicted gunshot wound. His associate, Joseph Williamson, would stand trial for the false imprisonment of dozens of men and the murder of several more, spanning a number of years. Many of the men were still receiving treatment to recover from injuries sustained while they were held captive. One captive, John Hall, remained in a critical condition.

I lay a bandaged hand on my chest; my heart was racing, then gradually calmed. The knot of tension slowly began loosening inside me. I opened my mouth to speak, but several doctors came into the room.

Jerry pushed himself to his feet. 'I'll leave you now,' he said. He lowered his head so that it was inches from mine.

'Everyone gets what they deserve in the end. And everyone gets a second chance. Don't blow yours Nathan.'

The bad news: I have multiple fractures in both legs from the impact of the van, and I also broke my arm when I fell out of the taxi. Concussion has made my memory of the accident very fuzzy. I am broken, inside and out.

The good news: a man called Jerry Foster saved me. Around 70,000 people in the UK alone share the surname Foster. Jerry is no relation to David. I am in no way associated with any of the prison scandal; Jerry has ensured that all my records were destroyed. He visits me regularly and provided me with a place to stay when I am eventually discharged. My journey to full recovery will be long and hard, but I have already started to heal.

Other titles by BLKDOG Publishing for your consideration:

Soul of a Vampire
By Silencio Marquez

Kris Kellman is a vampire living in Calgary, Canada who works as a detective at the Magical Laws Division. It's his job to solve crimes committed by magical people like himself. When his former lover, Zeke Yonah, shows up on his doorstep covered in blood and asking for help, Kris is conflicted. Is he a vampire first, or is he a cop?

As he begins to investigate the murder that Zeke doesn't remember committing, things get really complicated when Kris realizes that Zeke is being set up for murder.

Charles Anderson is in charge of the vampire community, and he has a plan to enslave all mankind. The only thing standing in his way are people like Zeke and Kris, a vampire whose loyalty can't be bought. Kris's ridiculous dragon-shifter boyfriend isn't making things easier either.

Kris realizes that if he can't stop Charles, it will mean war between humans and vampires. He knows that it's not just humans that will suffer, but vampires like him who won't just sit by and let Charles get away with genocide. Will Kris do what's right and bring Charles to justice before it's too late?

Diary of a Vigilante
By Shaun Curtis

One man's angel is another man's devil. One man's hero is another man's killer.

It's a blurred line between hero and villain, between vigilante and criminal, between decent citizen and maniac - and this is where Jack finds himself. Jack is a man haunted by the failures of a justice system he feels is broken and the seemingly arbitrary punishments measured out to those who have offended the state.

When his friend's family find themselves threatened by a sexual predator and let down by the police, Jack snaps, and a journey of vigilantism, anger and revenge pursues. Told from his point of view, the **Diary of a Vigilante**, Jack descends further into the pits of the underworld, and the man who set out to clean the streets, finds that *he* becomes the top target of law enforcement.

What price will Jack pay for his vengeance, and in a world of eye-for-an-eye justice, what sort of man will he be at the end? Will he become the very same monster he sought to destroy?

Arc City Stories
By various authors

Welcome to Arc City.

A city that exists in a world beyond governments, where war and climate change have destroyed the old order. Corporations are now the authorities of the surviving city states. The elite live in luxury above the clouds in their towers, everyone else lives further down, based on their corporate and economic worth.

Arc City Stories is an exciting, action-packed collection of nine cyberpunk tales, written by eight authors, of various citizens each trying to survive, in their own way, this brave new world.

Prester John
By Richard Denham

He sits on his jewelled throne on the Horn of Africa in the maps of the sixteenth century. He can see his whole empire reflected in a mirror outside his palace. He carries three crosses into battle and each cross is guarded by one hundred thousand men. He was with St Thomas in the third century when he set up a Christian church in India. He came like a thunderbolt out of the far East eight centuries later, to rescue the crusaders clinging on to Jerusalem. And he was still there when Portuguese explorers went looking for him in the fifteenth century.

But it was noticeable that as men looked outward, exploring more of the natural world; as science replaced superstition and the age of miracles faded, Prester John was always elsewhere. He was beyond the Mountains of the Moon, at the edge of the earth, near the mouth of Hell.

Was he real? Did he ever exist? This book will take you on a journey of a lifetime, to worlds that might have been, but never were. It will take you, if you are brave enough, into the world of Prester John.

**A Storm of Magic
By Ashley Laino**

Being brought back from the dead is an impressive trick, even for magician Darien Burron. Now he must try and use his sleight of hand to swindle modern-day witch, Mirah, to sign her power away, or end up a tormented demon in the afterlife.

Meanwhile, sixteen-year-old Mirah is starting to lose control of her powers. After an incident at her aunt's Witchery store, Mirah is sent to a secret coven to learn to control her abilities.

While away, Mirah meets up with a soft-spoken clairvoyant, a brazen storm witch, and the creator of dark magic itself. The young woman must learn to trust in herself before she loses herself entirely to the darkness that hunts her.

Consumed
By Justin Alcala

Sergeant Nathaniel Brannick is trapped in Victorian London during a period of disease, crime, and insatiable vices. One night, Brannick returns from work to find an eerie messenger in his flat who warns him of dark things to come.

When his next case involves a victim who suffered from consumption, he uncovers clues that lead him to believe the messenger's warning. Despite his incredulity, he can't help but wonder if the practical man he once was has been altered by an investigation encompassed in the paranormal. That is, until he meets the witch hunters, and everything takes a turn for the worse.

EST. 2019

BLKDOG

www.blkdogpublishing.com